CURTAIN CREEK FARM

Also by Nance Van Winckel

Fiction
Limited Lifetime Warranty
Quake

Poetry
Bad Girl, with Hawk
The Dirt
After a Spell

For Doniella,
So great to know
you here in Seattle at Hugo House.

CURTAIN CREEK FARM

Stories

all best,

Nance Van Winckel

Nance Van Winckel

6/11/00

A Karen and Michael Braziller Book

PERSEA BOOKS/ NEW YORK

For information, write to the publisher:
Persea Books, Inc.
171 Madison Avenue
New York, NY 10016

Library in Congress Cataloging-in-Publishing Data

Van Winckel, Nance.
Curtain Creek Farm : stories / Nance Van Winckel.
p. cm.
Contents: Sometimes he borrowed a horse — Immunity —
The land of anarchy—Making headway — Beside ourselves —
The lap of luxury — The expectation of abundance — Treat me nice.
ISBN 0-89255-250-6 (alk. paper)
1. Washington (State)—Social life and customs—Fiction.
2. Communal living—Fiction
I. Title.

PS3572.A546 C87 2000
813'.54— dc21
00-023712

Designed by Leah Lococo
Typeset in Adobe Garamond.
Manufactured in the United States of America
First Edition

CONTENTS

CURTAIN CREEK FARM

SOMETIMES HE BORROWED A HORSE

(Pauline)

Outside, the dogs were going crazy, mad to couple with wolves. Yowls and yip-yip-yip past the rooftops. Closer by, a baby cried. *What* baby? *Whose* baby?

Now I try to wake up and go to the child. Her cries are shrill. Get *up*, I'm calling from my waking self to my sleeping self. Just moments ago, a woman in khaki overalls, her eyebrows thick and gray, had been stirring a pot on a woodstove, her metal spoon going pfisk-pfisk, pfisk-pfisk. The venison smell still seems to linger in the air, in this air.

I open my eyes. School bus brakes squeal; children shout, and the dogs run barking after them. And the phone's ringing. More dread on the dread. Believing it's *him*, my cousin Mitch—no doubt on the lam again. Just wanting to check in, he'll say, before he heads back through the rock canyons, into the mountains, to sequester himself once more inside the mud walls, the solitary cell he loves.

*   *   *

All afternoon the Greyhound bus followed the jagged swath of the St. Joe River, hurtling past the tightly packed crossroads towns. Mitch had told me on the phone where I should meet him: just above Orofino, in Weippe, at the Timberline Café. At 6:25 a.m., when the bus got in. He said he wanted to give me something, but I had to come down there to Idaho and get it myself. He wouldn't say what or why. He claimed it wasn't something for little ears inside the phone wires to hear.

"If I'm going to bus myself that far in the middle of *March*," I said, "I need more info."

Mitch sighed into the nine hundred miles between us. "You know I wouldn't ask, Pauline, if it wasn't important."

Near sunset and with a light snow falling, the bus made a stopover in Harrison at The River Bend, a combination diner, bus depot, and post office. That's where, as I stood sipping a cup of tepid tea, I saw my cousin's face: a face almost obliterated, in the thumbnail photograph, by his thin pointed beard, dark hair, and heavy black glasses. But it was Mitch, all right—Mitch in a wanted poster.

"That boy ain't as dangerous as he looks, honey," a woman said suddenly.

I turned. Her hazel eyes, below a tall hive of yellow hair, were watching me through the postal window.

"You buying stamps? We're about to close."

I shook my head and looked again at the poster. Mitch stared back, his eyes full of the old fierceness I remembered from our childhood. So many ordinary events in the ordinary world seemed to baffle or offend him. I'd often wondered how his life might have turned out if something as simple as the date he'd almost had with Trudy Bledsoe had gone differently. What if Trudy *hadn't* laughed when he'd shown up at her door in a red bow tie? What if Mitch had been able to step for one second out of his new black oxfords and see what Trudy saw? Maybe he'd have realized how a bow tie for the youth dance at the Waupaca YMCA *could be* funny, and he'd have stuffed the tie in his pocket and gone off to the dance with Trudy. Over the years, a thousand small misdemeanors like this one could incubate into felonies. His face had grown leaner and his brown eyes blacker until he'd become that face in the poster.

Back on the bus, I stuffed the tuna sandwich I'd bought into my pack. The truth was Mitch's current troubles hardly seemed as bad as the earlier ones. The poster announced he was wanted for trespassing, destruction of property, breaking and entering, and for violating Department of Fish and Wildlife licensing ordinances. But there was no mention of poaching or of unlawful sales of pelts, crimes he'd already done time for—three years—in Utah. From jail, Mitch had sent me a newspaper article and accompanying photograph. His face was wider and tanner then, and clean-shaven. His ankles were in leg-irons. The article said he'd shot wild mustangs and used them as bait for trapping bobcats.

He'd also sent a postcard. *Western Jackalope, State Animal of Utah,* it said on the front beneath the rabbit with antlers and four hooves. On the back was Mitch's cramped printing: *This critter is NOT real.* As if I'd think a jackalope was. As if I lived in some nutty dream of the West.

*   *   *

Eight years ago, shortly after I moved to Curtain Creek Farm—or *Collective,* as it was called now on our website— Mitch had come to visit, or to lie low. Probably both. But he'd helped out. He'd strung fence around the cabbages to keep the skunks away. For a few months he fit right in.

He had arrived in a lavender Coupe de Ville, a car he claimed he'd bought for a hundred bucks off the gypsies in Boise. From there, Curtain Creek was a day's drive straight north, fifty miles past Spokane, thirty miles west of Idaho, and a stone's throw from Canada. Mountains, jagged and snow-capped, stood everywhere in between. Mitch found my place—a blue, single-car, aluminum garage—and honked. I stepped out of the side door. He waved, then revved the engine and drove right past me into the tall meadow grass. He turned off the ignition and left the keys dangling. "She don't have a single mile left in her," he said as he flung open the door.

That car is still where he'd left it, sun-bleached to a peachy pink. Its two doors on the passenger side are propped open, and the chickens—Leghorns and Silver-laced Columbians—fly in and out, flapping, following a rooster, in and out of the chicken Coupe de Ville. My sweet chickadoodles, I call to them, tossing potato peels, cooing back at their cooing.

It was summer when Mitch arrived. He laid a bedroll outside. To sleep beneath the blue yonder, he said. He'd brought the same Zane Greys he'd read as a boy. I recognized their titles—*Black Mesa, Desert Gold, The Border Legion.* In the books the West was savage but the cowboys were savvy. Which was all a crock, Mitch said. That West never existed. It was a hoax made up to give us a better history than the real one we'd barely survived, the one Mitch claimed we'd had no right to survive.

One afternoon Mitch got a ride into town in order to get himself "an honest-to-God hamburger." He'd had as much as he could stomach of the Farm's vegetarian cuisine. When he returned, walking briskly up our gravel road, he was carrying a rifle, its shiny steel barrel propped nonchalantly on his shoulder. This rankled my neighbors.

Rollie came down my driveway, with Scooter and Don right behind him.

"Not *here,* okay? We're not about violence," Rollie said. Don smiled at Mitch, flashing his two dark teeth, then shrugged like he'd rather be elsewhere. Scooter just stared at the rifle as if expecting it to disappear now.

"He knows," I said. "I've explained it."

Mitch held out the gun for them to examine. "It's a Winchester, a classic. It's got a hexagonal barrel."

Rollie, who was maybe seventy and certainly the oldest of us at the Farm, took off his ragged straw hat. Beneath it, wrapped around his forehead, was a faded blue bandanna that he yanked up and down to wipe away the sweat. Then he nodded once at the rifle. "Whatever we can make happen out here, it won't be because of those."

"You got porcupines chewing up your fruit trees. I can fix that," Mitch said. But Scooter and Don had already begun walking away.

"*Adios*," Rollie said, holding Mitch's eyes. Then he turned and put the hat back on.

"Hey," Mitch shouted after them, "I can shoot the red off a woodpecker from a hundred yards."

I'd heard him say that last part before. It was a boast he'd picked up as a teenager back in Wisconsin, from Mr. Bidecki, a mink farmer. It was Mr. Bidecki I blamed for setting Mitch off down this road of weapons and bloody, bug-eyed animals. He'd taught Mitch how to zap the minks with a prod, then quickly slit their throats and skin them. I still remember their chilling little high-pitched squeals when the prod hit.

Our two fathers, who were brothers, didn't like this killing business either. They were Quakers. Still, when Mitch brought home a venison roast and Uncle Milt cooked it up, we all passed the platter around. My father, his jaw grinding slowly through the black meat, frowned as he chewed. But when the platter came around again, he'd have another helping and ladle on the dark gravy.

"The gun's *not* negotiable," I told Mitch when my neighbors left. "It's a strict rule. So don't even think about arguing."

"What the hell kind of freedom do you call this, Pauline?" He shook his head. "I don't get it."

After the bus dropped me in Weippe, I headed for the café. Immediately Mitch appeared, stepping out of the trees. His small frame was hunched, his head covered by the hood of a maroon poncho.

"We came through a lot of snow," I said.

"That's a good bus. It most always gets through." He stood off a few feet, his face expressionless, his chin pulled down like a question mark by the tip of his beard. Then he yanked on a rope at his shoulder and produced a pair of snow-shoes. "You're going to need these." He set them near my feet.

I saw he had on a pair, too. Behind him the sunrise had reddened the edge of the high mountain prairie above Orofino and the Clearwater River. Mitch watched me buckle the straps over my boots. When I'd taken a clumsy step forward, he nod-ded at the snowshoes as if they themselves held the secrets to this whole venture through hip-high snow to who knew where.

From Weippe we slogged all day up powdery drifts east to Chamook Ridge, three thousand feet up, to a small ranger cabin. Then, wrapped in blankets, we sat on the floor. I could still see my breath, even though a tiny fire had been glowing for an hour. Mitch lit a couple of candles and put them between us.

"Would they shoot you, Mitch? If they came in here right now?"

His eyes pinched together; his thin lips parted slightly. "They wouldn't do that. No. Not unless I put a gun in their faces." He banked a few coals onto the hearth.

"Which you wouldn't do." I watched him lean over the wood scraps. "Right?"

He shrugged. "Shake it off, Pauline. It's a hot-damn beautiful evening."

If the weather held, Mitch said, tomorrow we'd go back down the other side of the ridge. Down there, he had something to show me, something he knew I'd like.

From under a three-legged coffee table, he pulled out a cardboard box and flipped the lid open. "See if there's anything in here you want."

I leaned forward and felt the muscles in my back tense. I winced.

"You're out of shape, aren't you?"

"I'm sorry."

Mitch reached into the box and lifted out a silver cookie tin. "This ain't what you think." He pulled off the top. "Look. It's raisins."

I was going with the program, I told myself. I didn't even look inside the tin. I just stuck my hand in and pulled out a little raisin box. In another cookie tin were bags of nuts. Mitch had set a kettle brewing on the banked coals. In no time we were drinking herb tea.

"You never know what-all you'll find in these places. I once got me a Buddha statue." He closed his eyes, squinting, remembering more. "A radio-controlled airplane. A trumpet. A deck of nudie cards." These spoils were all part of the sport for Mitch, a contest full of covert excursions into the civilized world. He busted out ranger station windows, picked locks. He'd step briefly into that world, partake of the pleasures there, and be gone.

As kids in Waupaca we'd played a game called Risk. We scattered armies across the countries of the globe, which lay flattened on a board in Mitch's basement. We launched missiles and positioned battleships. Mitch made machine-gun sounds in his throat when he invaded my tiny blue island of Tonga or Banaba. The world was his if the dice fell his way. And they always did. My countries cowered before his black tanks.

That's how I felt now in the Chamook ranger station: under siege. I saw all his guns—no doubt stolen from other ranger stations—propped neatly against a wall. Boxes of shiny shells lay spilled open in a corner near his bedroll.

"You've got everything you need, don't you?"

He passed me a strip of dried venison. "I just shoot what I can eat." He pulled off the maroon poncho. Underneath was a down parka. As the air inside the cabin slowly lost its icy edge, his face grew whiter. He couldn't have weighed more than 130 pounds, a little less than I weighed. His chest and neck were thin, his hair damp and matted to his skull.

As I sucked the salty, bitter venison, Mitch told me how a sheriff had tracked him through High Horse Pass and all the way to a hunting lodge near Downy Butte. But by the time the sheriff got there, Mitch had pilfered a flashlight and binoculars and was long gone. Then an elk hunter had seen him near Skull Creek, where Mitch had gone into another ranger cabin, shaved with the ranger's gear, and stolen the maroon poncho. The hunter who'd seen him hadn't thought to mention it to the sheriff's office for a couple of days, which only proved, Mitch said, that the people liked him.

"Where'd your hair go?" he asked when I finally took off my ski hat.

I shrugged and raked it back with my fingers. I'd cut it myself: short. No frills, no fuss, I was going to tell him, but he'd already turned his attention to other matters. From his coat pocket he took out and unfolded a newspaper article, then handed it to me. I bent near the candle. "Sticky-Fingered Mountain Man Strikes Again," the headline read. I skimmed through the description of his exploits to the last sentence: "If the weather isn't horrendous, the renegade has been known to borrow a horse."

I stretched my legs in front of me and smiled at him. "You've certainly figured out how to forage in this forest."

He nodded, took the clipping back, and refolded it carefully along its fold lines. "There's plenty everywhere." He swept an arm around the room. "So much it won't even be missed."

Clearly Mitch didn't think of himself as a criminal. He meant no one harm. He posed no danger. What he thought the world wanted from him was his participation in it. So he'd devised his own way to oblige, a way to intersect his life with other people's lives, with their world. To him, this was a good thing: a transaction, an interchange.

The herb tea had made me sleepy. The last thing I saw, before I lay back and pulled a blanket on top of me, was

Mitch taking off his black boots and unwinding what looked like dishtowels from his feet.

*   *   *

The next day at sunup we headed to what I supposed was another ranger's cabin. Augie's place, Mitch called it. Our snowshoes imprinted diamond grids as we side-stepped along the packed snow of the canyon's switchbacks, trails mule deer and elk had made, coming down to shove their snouts through the thin river ice for a drink. We saw their hoofprints mingled in the snow. Warming ourselves for a moment in a sunny spot, we watched our breaths billow.

"You should get in shape, Pauly," Mitch said, then looked off as if he hadn't spoken.

"It's not like I'm out here every day in this thin air."

He glanced behind him. "The sheriff's got himself a high-powered spotting scope." He nodded to me as if I should have known that.

"Look, Mitch. I'm not going to travel on and on with you like this, like an accomplice."

"No need to think in those terms. We'll just shoot what we can eat."

"*We?* I'm not shooting anything."

He pulled at his beard, then reached in his poncho pocket. "Pauly, I need new ones of these."

I leaned toward him. He put a pair of eyeglasses in my hand. One of the lenses was badly shattered.

"I wouldn't cause any trouble up there at the commune," he said suddenly. "I'm not with the guns anymore."

"What about all those back at the cabin?"

"They're *staying*. I'm *going*."

"I don't think so, Mitch. I don't think it would work."

Then he outlined his plan. He'd learned a new skill, he said, a brand-new trade. Raising some very special dogs.

"We've already got dogs at the Farm. Lots of dogs."

"Not like these." He shook his head. "These are hot-damn wild dogs. You'll see. It would be a going thing up there."

He jerked his mittens off, bent down, and cinched up a loose strap on my snowshoe. "How's that?"

"Good. That's good."

I closed my hands around the eyeglasses. They seemed like a sad offering he'd made to me. As I put them in my pocket, I remembered another pathetic thing he'd handed me years ago in Waupaca: that red bow tie he'd tried to wear to the YMCA dance. After Trudy Bledsoe had closed her door on Mitch, he'd wandered around for a few hours, then appeared on my porch.

"Your goofy cousin's out there," my mother said, peering out the window, her nose between our parted curtains. I'd been home from the dance myself for only ten minutes, and I was just settling in, watching Johnny Carson with my father on the couch.

"Honestly," my mother said, "he doesn't knock or anything. He just sits there." Back then, in 1970, there were singular, specific reactions expected for every action done for us, or to us, in the world. I was fifteen and Mitch was seventeen, and his disdain for this worldview was already becoming clear.

At the mixer I'd danced with Frank Gunther who, in two more years, would be stacking sandbags in Cambodia where a bullet through his neck—the very neck I'd just been breathing on—would take him down. In the Y's small auditorium there was an odor of sweat. Frank Gunther pulled me close as we danced to a slow song, the Righteous Brothers singing about how they couldn't go on, but they obviously *were.*

Through the whole long song, I felt Frank's breath against my cheek. He said nothing, but his hands, low on my back, were almost pleading. Near the end of the song, he was moving his groin against me, and at first, dizzy and distracted by the rank air, I didn't realize what part of him it was that was so warm, urgent, and large between us. And then I did. I sucked in my breath when I knew, when I realized that such desire could happen right there, at a mixer, at the Y on Murdock Street. I stroked Frank's neck. The couples whirled around us. The center of our bodies felt ionized. We held down the center of the dance floor.

Then I'd come home to find my cousin Mitch on the porch step. He had the red bow tie in his hand. "Pauline," he said, "I can't do this. I can't." He handed it to me.

I clamped the bow tie in my hair like a barrette.

"Don't." He reached toward it. "Don't horse around like that."

I put it back in his hand. "You've got loads of potential," I told him, which was a thing my mother always said. Mitch's own mother was dead—killed by a fire that swept through their house while he was in his first-grade class. One day he'd come home from school to a pile of ashes and his father weeping.

"You've got a true talent for *something*," I went on in my mother's voice, and with my hand on my hip in the exact same way she used to stand in the kitchen talking to me. "You've got to find out what it is and let it take you."

Neither of us could have known then how the belief in this lie—in some single true talent streaming toward us—would send us helter-skelter to the four winds. At a school in Salt Lake I'd tried modern dance. Next I'd been a dealer in Reno, then a night-shift stock girl at a Spokane Safeway. And for the last eight years I'd been feeding the Farm's chickens, lifting out trays of honey from the beehives, and cutting the children's hair. I had battery-powered shears and four pair of barbering scissors. And although I'd never officially learned how, I could do the job well enough. I'd even hung out a business sign: an old pair of rusty grass clippers. *Kwick*, I'd painted in black on one blade, and *Kuts* on the other. Still, sometimes I thought about the True Talent Express: a long silver train speeding past in the distance, the blast of its whistle as it goes by.

* * *

As Mitch and I hiked with our faces in the sun, I settled into the rhythm of my snowshoes whisking over snow. I ate my tuna sandwich, although Mitch kept us walking. The bread was half-frozen so I had to suck each bite before I chewed. I walked in a quiet that had the feel of our old Quaker meetings, our silent circle. There, in matching red suspenders, our two fathers would bow their heads. They might have been asleep. They might have been enraptured in the Lord. Mitch and I, sitting among the grownups, waited for the holiness to make its way into our hearts. Everyone would squirm for a while before we settled into the quiet and felt the world slip away. "Just let it fade on out, Pauline," my father used to say. "It's a lovely thing when it does." But from beyond the window, I'd hear children playing—a girl's soft, steady counting. Then her shout would puncture our silence: "Okay, ready or not, here I come!"

"Are they still calling themselves *anarchists* out there at the Farm?" Mitch asked me. We'd begun side-stepping our way downward, toward a creek. Pine boughs smacked our faces and dumped snow on our shoulders.

I watched his legs' graceful maneuvering and tried to match his strides. In my eight years at Curtain Creek, I'd learned a few responses to this question. "Anarchy doesn't have to mean cities in flames," I said. "It doesn't have to mean assassination and bombs and looting." I watched him a few yards below me, planting one leg then another down hard. "We're trying for something that's maybe impossible. We're our own guinea pigs."

"Guinea pigs." Mitch took another step and stopped.

"Order without laws," I went on. "We don't know if

that's possible. Order from within, not from without. We're trying to see if it works."

"Just that one law," he said softly, as if to himself.

I stepped as best I could into his prints, following them down. In their clumsy wooden snowshoes, my feet felt like stones roped to sticks. I flung them out into Mitch's prints. To anyone trailing us, which was not an unreasonable thought, our path would have appeared the path of one person, a sloppy climber, sliding and slipping.

*   *   *

It was hopeless trying to sleep. Outside, dogs were howling. The dogs had been cross-bred with wolves, or, more likely, I thought when I saw them, wolves crossed with dogs. From their long gleaming teeth dangled streams of drool. The dogs padded around, yipping. "They're fretting," Augie would say later. "Not used to strangers." Meaning me.

I lay in a heap of smelly blankets, thinking I was dreaming and dreaming I was sleeping. I'd been too tired to eat, too tired to ask questions, too tired from all the slogging—sunup to sundown on those horrid snowshoes—to try to figure out what was going on here.

"Only tonight then," I heard Augie say to Mitch. "I don't want trouble."

Even before Augie's place had come into view from the creek path, Mitch and I had heard the dogs, and they'd heard us. Augie's place was a plywood-and-aluminum hut tipped precariously against a granite cliff, and strung against the hut was the dogs' pen: heavy wire fence on top, the rock cliff in back.

"I'm not going near those dogs," I said. "They look like they want to kill us."

"Yeah, they probably do." Mitch unlaced his snowshoes, then mine. I put my mittened hand on his head to steady myself when he knelt down. I was shivering, my thighs aching. The dogs yowled and lunged at the fence.

Mitch pushed open the door of the lean-to. Inside, it was almost as dark as it had been outside. Augie, sitting in the only chair, a rocker, didn't look up when we came in.

"Close the door good," Augie said, and I froze. It was a woman's voice. A *woman*. A dark blue knit cap covered her hair.

Mitch steered me toward a table, where a kerosene lamp emitted an amber light. Near the lamp was a skillet piled high with yellow bones.

"There's hot stew on the stove," Augie said. "Y'all can help yourself."

Just then, from a corner, a baby cried. I looked quickly at Mitch, who was already ladling dark red stew into a bowl. "Mitch?" I said softly. I slipped off my mittens. I still had on my parka and boots. "Mitch?"

He wouldn't look at me. He took a step and handed me the bowl. Then he pulled open a drawer in the table, took out two spoons, and held one toward me, not letting his eyes meet mine, acting busy with his task. I stared at him.

The baby's cries grew louder. Mitch jabbed the spoon

into my bowl and moved back to the stove. Watching only the path of his own spoon, he ate directly from the pot.

Augie got up and went to the door. She stepped outside. "It's all right," she shouted at the dogs. "Pipe down." And amazingly, they did. The baby, too.

When Augie came back, she moved toward us. She wore a pair of khaki overalls. A blue wool blanket, full of holes, was safety-pinned at her neck like a shawl. With a big metal spoon she stirred the stew on the woodstove, which was an old oil drum. Augie's face was that of a young woman's, smooth and clear, but her eyebrows were two dense, gray crescents.

Mitch took a jar of jam from his coat pocket and held it out to her.

Not touching it, but bending close, she read the label. "Apricot," she said. Then she glanced at me, and though I can't be sure, I thought she winked. Not smiling. Almost more a tic than a wink.

Mitch set the jam on the table. I felt lost, dizzy in the questions whirling through my head. My mouth felt too dry to speak. I could only stand there, watching.

"Pauline's tired," Mitch said to Augie. Then he turned to me and took the bowl, which had been warming my hands. "Rest over there for a while." He nodded behind me. "You can eat this later. Venison stew. You like that. Remember?"

In a corner I rolled myself into the blankets on the dirt floor. The muscles in my calves throbbed. I realized when I was wrapped and warm that I was beyond tired.

The words my mind wanted to ask fell through my mouth as moans, sighs.

From out of the smoke and shadows, Augie moved toward the wooden apple crate that held the baby. She put her hand in there. "It's all right then," she said. "Never mind."

I heard Mitch, still by the stove, saying something about a sheriff and the spotting scope and Augie saying again how she didn't want trouble. Her metal spoon went pfisk-pfisk, pfisk-pfisk.

The dogs barked off and on. I closed my eyes. In my dream kids played hide-and-seek outside our Quaker meeting, while inside we sat waiting, trying to push back at the trees scraping the window in the spring breezes. But then, No, I thought in the dream, maybe that's the High Holiness Himself. I stared into the leaf buds. I felt the light in them, felt its warmth wavering, leaking into me. And from far off came some calling: "Ollie, ollie, ox-in-free."

*   *   *

Five months later, the baby, Mitch's baby, sits next to me in a diner. It's as if the trek through the woods never happened, couldn't have happened. I'm back in Wisconsin for my mother's funeral. It's full-blown fall in the Midwest and my father and Uncle Milt are in their glory among the auburn corn fields. We've driven downtown, and they sit across from me and the baby over their blue-plate specials of white food—chicken-fried steaks, milk gravy, and biscuits.

"We're right smack dab in the middle of the Knudsens' hog farm," my father says.

Uncle Milt glances out the window behind me, then shakes his head. "Nope. Don't think so." He lifts a forkful of biscuit to his mouth and bites off half. "That was farther down the road."

"Yeah, yeah, yeah," my father says in a rush, which the baby immediately begins to mimic, softly, her head against my left arm, mumbling "Yeff, yeff, yeff."

"He's right." My father nods to Uncle Milt. "We're at the exact spot where the Knudsens' chicken coop was. Right where they had those awful chickens."

"Those Knudsens never took care of their chickens," Uncle Milt offers. "That was the smellingest hen house in the county."

"Your mother went to school with that Knudsen girl, what was her name?" My father's question seems addressed to me, although I've never heard of these people, of their farm.

"Dad, we're in a damned Denny's, for Pete's sake. On Spring Street." I put my head back against the window ledge, the window through which the past and present are apparently streaming like two rivers through a confluence. I tear open a cellophane package and hand the baby, Suzanne, a saltine. I gave her that name a few days after I'd brought her back to the Farm. Suzanne—after Mitch's mother. She likes the name and knows it's hers. She holds up her two little fists and shakes them when someone says it.

My father and his brother could almost be twins—tall and slim, their similar stoops when they stand. They wear pastel shirts, and my father's torso seems sliced vertically into thirds by his new navy suspenders, as does Uncle Milt's by his old red ones.

I hadn't given them any warning about the baby. I'd decided just to bring her and explain it all when I got here. Besides, I hadn't known what to say to my father in the thick of our grief on the phone. His call hadn't come at a good moment. Outside, the dogs had been barking, the kids shouting and jumping off the school bus, and the baby and I had just been waking from our naps. Half in a dream, I'd thought it was going to be Mitch. Then there was my father's voice, trembling. No one had expected my mother to be the first to go, for her heart to shut down as she sat shucking corn on the back porch before dinner.

At the Milwaukee airport, the two men had stared at the baby, sixteen months old now and asleep finally, after the long flight, in my arms. At last my father smiled at me. "Good-looking baby."

We were waiting by the carousel for my suitcase. "Suzanne, this is your grandfather," I whispered to her and nodded to Uncle Milt.

"You don't mean me, darlin'." He grinned at my father.

Then they both leaned forward. "What?" Uncle Milt said.

"That's right. She's Mitch's. I'm just baby-sitting for a while. Till Mitch gets back on his feet."

Uncle Milt slowly aimed his large brown index finger toward the baby's face, stopping it carefully against her bright ruddy cheek. Then he laughed.

I'd greatly overprepared the story, I discovered. As we drove south through the honey-colored corn stubble and then west into the low, rolling hills toward Waupaca, the brothers in the front seat asked few questions and, in fact, seemed hardly to be listening to me. They kept interrupting to tell me what once had stood where now there was a motel or a shopping mall—the so-and-sos' farm, the county dump. In the backseat with the baby belted in, asleep with her head in my lap, I kept sending forward pieces of my story, Mitch's story, with my own careful spin. My father and uncle nodded as if I were giving a report on a book I'd read. "He has a girlfriend," I told them. "Augie. She's a professional dog breeder. They're trying to run this business together. So I'm just looking after Suzanne for a year or two. Till they get themselves established."

"They're not married?" My father opened the window an inch, so I had to answer over a rush of wind.

"They'll probably do that. Eventually."

"I never thought he'd *ever* have a girlfriend," Uncle Milt said to the alfalfa field passing on our right.

"Is this too much air for anyone?" my father asked, catching my eye in the rearview mirror, and I shook my head.

I had other chapters of the story made up and ready to go. Things to tell them about Augie. "She's a strong, independent woman," I was going to say. I had some, but not all, of the truth to give them about Mitch. "He's on probation now, a work-release program, painting ranger cabins."

"Us two made a mistake," Mitch had said that morning as we'd prepared to leave Augie's. "We won't do that anymore."

"What's her name?" I'd asked when Augie put the child in my arms. The baby stared up at me, blinking.

Augie shrugged. She handed me a Coke bottle of milk, capped by a brown nipple. "I had me a baby once before. Years ago." She looked at Mitch. "Not *his*. And some people came and took it away. There was trouble. Trouble for a long time." She shook her head and tucked the baby's arms inside the blanket. "I can't have that again."

"I'm just not sure," I kept saying. But it didn't seem I was being asked. No question was ever put to me.

"This baby's got no papers," Mitch said as we went outside.

Augie pulled a tarp off a snowmobile and handed Mitch the key. "I wrote my post office address on this if you need me to sign something." She shoved a piece of cardboard into a pocket of my knapsack. "I'll be up to Weippe for mail in late May. I don't mind signing. If you need that." She nodded to Mitch, who'd already climbed on the snowmobile. "Him either. He'll sign."

Mitch sat looking at the key in his hand. Then he stuck it in the ignition. I got on behind him and put the baby between us.

Days later, back at the Farm with Suzanne, I'd opened my door to find a baby stroller: inside it, five baby bottles, two dozen carefully washed and folded diapers, and jars of home-canned applesauce and mashed carrots. For Mitch, the world of people coming and going was an incomprehensible chaos; societal rules had come to seem arbitrary, laws capricious, and family bonds enigmatic. But at the Farm, I'd learned to feel a secret pulse of order. Like the bubbling tumult of Curtain Creek itself that ran down the middle of our canyon. A sense within the nonsense.

When Rollie, Scooter, and Don—the three emissaries on their information-gathering mission—appeared at my door, they met my curious answers to their questions with their customary nonchalance.

"Nope," I said, "nope, she doesn't have a birth certificate."

"Well." Rollie bent down and handed Suzanne a clothespin doll. "We can handle that, Pauline." He smiled. The baby put the clothespin head in her mouth.

"Should we put *you* as the mother?" Don asked.

Scooter took a small square pad of yellow sticky-notes and a pencil stub from his Hawaiian shirt pocket. "Maybe we should write this down."

Don rolled his eyes.

"Yeah, you can put me. That's a lie, though. Is that all right?"

Don, Scooter, and I looked at Rollie, who kept watching the baby but nodded. Then Scooter wrote down PAULINE METCALF, MOTHER in big block letters, and Don flashed his black-holed smile.

"This baby has the biggest brown eyes I've ever seen,"

the waitress at Denny's says as she sets down our three plates of apple pie. She puts a bowl of vanilla ice cream in front of Suzanne and stands grinning beneficently over us.

"This is our grandbaby," my father tells her.

Uncle Milt nods and pushes the ice cream closer to the baby.

"Well, isn't that something." The waitress slowly turns toward the long counter behind her. "Hey, Sonia, come over here. You have to see Conrad and Milt's grandbaby."

Suzanne jabs her spoon into the middle of the ice cream. "Scream," she calls it.

My father and Uncle Milt beam. Apparently, in Denny's, among the white food and white plates, the two waitresses talking baby-talk to Suzanne need no explanation about how two brothers can both be a child's grandfather—which, in a way, they are.

When my father asks the waitresses if they realize they're standing smack dab in the middle of the Knudsens' chicken farm, the women just smile and shake their heads. And outside our window, the chicken coop that's been gone for thirty years stands again, before us. The hens squawk. I imagine their wings striking the glass.

Yesterday, I'd taken Suzanne to my father's neighbor, Harriet, who'd offered to watch her while my mother's memorial service was held. Twenty people, their faces tanned and creased by the long summer of work outdoors, sat in a circle with their heads bowed. My father sat beside me, his large square hands folded. I felt his chest rise and fall with the effort of deep breaths, an effort not to let his grief overtake him as a few people among the group spoke of my mother. "She searched for the good in everyone. She never dwelt on the bad." I pressed my father's hand. Across the circle, Uncle Milt smiled at us, nodded, and closed his eyes. The leaves beyond the window were golden on the now-huge maple. Someone remembered a winter coat my mother had given her years ago during the war. The voices of remembering grew softer.

Then the silence came. Oddly, with the sun on my face, I was happy. Even in my tears. What I'd come to see was that it didn't matter if any talent ever found us, ever claimed us, since enough else—arising wondrously from nowhere—did. I let myself slip down into the circle's quiet. I was crossing a frozen stream behind my wild cousin, holding out my arms, sliding my snowshoes across the ice, and I was watching a toddler chase a red chicken toward a car so overgrown with weeds, it hardly seemed a car anymore. "My sweet chickadoodles," I called; then ". . . three, four, five," I was counting eggs into a basket. And ". . . eight, nine, ten, here I come, ready or not," a child was shouting. Someone yelled to a dog down the road to "pipe down." And "Pauline," my mother says, her hands on her hips, "Pauline, your goofy cousin's outside. Just sitting there. He's waiting for you. Go on out there and see what he wants." And I do. I always do.

IMMUNITY

(Marnie)

Outside Ivy's living room window—with the river valley below spongy and blue-green from days of rain—Ivy's brother Randall vaults past us, arms over his head. He spurts up like a geyser from the valley, then sinks back down, out of sight.

Ivy sees me watching him. "Dweeb." She rolls her eyes toward the window. "When this TV show's over, his turn's done. He's history."

On the TV a baby spits something green at a man, and the whites of the man's eyes widen beneath the goop. Then come peals of laughter. "Who's that laughing?" I ask Ivy.

"The studio audience." She turns, juts her chin out. "Duh-uh."

"The *heck* it is," Ivy's mother shouts from the kitchen. "That's a laugh track, girls."

Ivy shrugs at the TV, and I glance out the window again at Randall, airborne. I hear the soft thud on the trampoline when he touches down.

"Surely you people out there on the commune have televisions?" Ivy's grandfather asks.

I turn, about to paste on a smile and say what I'm supposed to—that we call it an *intentional community*, mister— but I don't. I'm sick of that. The grandfather sits on the sofa, his feet in crimson slippers on a leather footstool.

"My father has a TV," I say. "With AM/FM radio."

The old man nods. The toes of his slippers jerk to the TV music. "Ivy, go fill this up for your old Pops like a good girl." He hands her a blue coffee mug.

She takes it but doesn't move. The TV laughter increases as more baby spit appears to ooze down the screen's backside until the whole picture's puke green. Then a commercial comes on for the number-one painkiller in America. On my father's portable TV, which is smaller than a toaster, all I've ever seen are football games and *Wall Street Week in Review*. "In a pig's eye!" my father likes to shout at the smirking, white-haired, stock-market man. "Keep your mitts off that thing, Marnie," my mother whispers when we see my father unload the TV from his van for one of his Saturday-night visits—with *me*, and not with her.

I follow Ivy into the kitchen and try not to act too interested as she presses the coffee mug against a button on the refrigerator and three ice cubes plunk out. Mrs. Martin is peeling an onion. I notice her apron and smile. "Did Ivy sew that?"

Mrs. Martin nods and wipes her fingers on the apron. "You do eat chicken, don't you, Marnie?"

"Sure."

"I've sewed way better stuff since then," Ivy says. The apron is blue cotton with white stars. Scallops of red lace are sewn along the bottom. It's exactly the sort of apron I know I'll have to make next year in sixth-grade Home Ec. Starched and ironed, the sample aprons hang above a chart of the five food groups. I have fifth-grade art in that room this year, which is almost as lame, with our pie-dough people baked stiff in a white oven. Already my person's spindly hands have snapped off so that with his sharply carved smile—an ear-to-ear crevice—he looks completely whacko, and seems to be waving those wrist stumps to flaunt it.

Ivy goes to the counter, tips a bottle of gin over the mug, then returns to the fridge and presses another button, which sends down a stream of water.

"You girls can sit down if you want," her grandfather says after Ivy's passed him the cup and we're standing in front of the TV again.

But we don't. All around our feet are sections of her brother's model-car race-track: black plastic straightaways, slopes, snaky curves. Fist-sized cars lie strewn about as if blown off the road by a hurricane. Beyond Ivy's window the wet pastureland shimmers. A few hours ago, riding out of town on her school bus, a cleaner yellow one that goes in the opposite direction from my own bus, I saw a few stupid cows that looked stuck, ankle-deep in the mosquito-filled meadow muck. Suddenly, high above all this green, Randall's white legs, snapped loose from his tuck and flip, go shooting up.

*   *   *

Finally on the trampoline, I aim myself at a lizard-shaped cloud straight overhead.

"Use your arms, Marnie," Ivy calls from above me. "For thrust. See." She whomps down, then throws her arms over her head as she springs up. "Like. This."

Getting in synch with Ivy, I bend my knees, hit the mat, and am launched like a cannonball toward the one-eyed cloud.

Ivy bounces in her own sector of sky, firing off questions about Wade Brooker: "Does he ever ask about me? Who does he talk to on the bus? Is he good at softball?"

I'm trying to practice my lift-off, get that thing with my arms. I fly so far up, eye to eye with the lizard-cloud, that when I glance down all I can say is "Whoa." My feet sail past the big window, where there's a flash of red slippers inside. "Whoa," I say again, softly, hoping Ivy can't tell I'm a little afraid now. I'm going too high and without the slightest idea of how to stop.

"Have you ever seen him talking to any girls?"

I shake my head. Her beloved Wade Brooker and I had one of our longest conversations while standing in our underpants. Of course we were only seven. We'd run inside the Farm's community lodge, but then I'd come to a standstill by a shower. I wouldn't go in. Black widow spiders prowled near the drain. "Don't worry, Marnie. They'll *move*." Brooker turned on the water, hard. This all happened a couple of years before my father hooked up a lime-green shower stall in our kitchen. And okay, the spiders did move. They skittered into a corner. But I just stared at Brooker. We'd been swimming and had been told to rinse off the pond bugs. But I'd take those itchy no-see-ums any day, I told him, over black widow bites.

"Those spiders can *kill* you," I said. We watched one tilt up her back with its iridescent red number eight. "She'll eat her husband's head off after they have S-E-X."

Brooker stepped into the shower. "Marnie, you need to get bitten a few times, don't you know that?" The spiders, in a crazy dance to stay outside the water's spray, flailed and slid off the shower walls. "So you build up an immunity. Then you won't have a single reason to be scared of them."

"Does he ever pitch?" Ivy wants to know. We're face to face, bouncing upward. "Bend your knees more," she says as we glide down.

And Ha! I want to say about the very idea of Wade Brooker lofting a pitch slowly and gently over home plate. Sunday afternoons at the Farm, almost everyone plays—little kids, parents, goofy visitors in their plastic flip-flops. But not Brooker. The boy Ivy loves has painted an empty propane tank cobalt blue, then mounted old truck springs, vertically, on top. These are antennae. Near them is a hole Brooker and his pals climb in and out of, a hole made years ago in a midnight explosion behind Brooker's house. This entire contraption is a spaceship, but I don't mention that to Ivy. "Yeah," is what I tell her. "Yeah, he's really good at softball."

"I love how tan his arms are. Already. He's smart, isn't he?" Ivy's black hair, when she jets down, streams above her head, then refolds into its perfect pageboy as she launches up again.

"Uh-huh. Super smart." I bend my knees, touch down, and shoot past her. I try to stay in a straight line between the trampoline and my white cloud, which hovers patiently as if waiting to suck me in. No side-tracking, I tell myself. No veering out past the circumference of silver springs that go *boing, boing.* Outside them is the no-space, the nothingness old sea captains believed they'd come to, where the squared-off edges of ocean, land, sky—everything—stopped, just plain stopped.

*   *   *

"Okay," my mother said as I was tying my sneakers this morning, "let's go over the words you're *not* going to say at Ivy's house."

"Fuck," I said. "Shit."

"Good." My mother nodded and put a sandwich in my backpack.

"Asshole. Piss-brain."

"Excellent, sweetie." She took a lumpy, hand-rolled ciga-rette from her shirt pocket and held it up in the air—her baton.

Seeing the yellow school bus swirl dust up the road, I rattled off the rest in a hurry, my mother beating time with the yellow cigarette to each word. Then she brushed my cheek with her hand. "Nicely done, Marnie."

All through dinner—we're eating a dish Ivy's mother

calls Chicken Divan—I don't let slip a single one of the words. Randall makes car engine sounds as he forks up green beans mixed with red things—*pimentos*, Ivy tells me.

After we've cleared the table, we go upstairs to Ivy's mother's private bathroom, where Ivy gives me a makeover. I sit on a white-cushioned stool while she plugs in a curling wand and hot rollers.

"Okay, first mousse." She shakes a silver canister, and as she does, she squinches her mouth and eyes into an expression of disgust. Into her palm she squirts a white mound of foam that puffs out like a frog's bulging throat. Ivy's read magazines. She's studied these things. She wears her hair a different way every day. She has barrettes and clips that part and twist its shining black mass, making waves, ridges.

"You should have bangs," she tells my face in the mirror. "Your forehead's too high." Grimacing again, she shakes a tall green bottle like it's a jug of orange juice. "All right. Now we're ready for volumizer."

At home my mother has none of these things. She wears her hair in either a single fat braid or two long ones down her back. Some days she sticks a red poppy behind her ear. But if she hands me one for my hair, I just shake my head. "Be sweet, sweetie" is what she tells me. *Be sweet. Be sweet.*

"The Farm's a world away from the world," my father says sometimes when we're walking up Canyon Road. He'll put his hand in my hair. "But I can't say it's a bad world, honey. I wish I could, but I can't." This summer he'll marry a woman I've never met named Christine. They'll live in his red brick house in Spokane, and—my mother's sure—fire off a new baby or two.

Sometimes when we're walking, he stops and points to the propane tank out by the log piles. "How's the space-ship coming?"

I shrug. "How should *I* know?"

We stand and watch the boys climb in and out of it. Brooker, pacing and wearing his baseball cap backwards, gives stern orders. Last week they attached a silver hubcap to the front end, calling it a heat shield.

On the school bus no one can help overhearing Wade Brooker's intensely boring lectures. "Gentlemen," he always starts as if he's Mr. Odeen, the sixth-grade history teacher. "Gentlemen, the electrodes in my headgear will feed me cru-cial flight data—altitude, warp speed, engine temperature. Then I'll make adjustments. I'll just *think* them. And *voilà*. From my head—straight into the navigational monitors. It's error-proof, gentlemen."

"That boy's got *ideas*," my mother told our neighbor Sonny, the sheep-lady, who said she'd heard that Wade was seeing our school's guidance counselor. Shoving her thick glasses higher on her nose, Sonny looked out our window toward Brooker's house, a hunched aluminum Quonset with a door that pulled up and down like the one on Ivy's garage. "I'm not surprised," my mother said, and I knew that what she meant to say but felt it wasn't her place to was, Well, *no wonder*—what with that loony Leonard for a father.

Mr. Brooker, she'd told me, was something of a hermit.

Which, she'd added quickly, he had every right to be. "A person has as much freedom as he's willing to take." That was a thing my mother liked to say. Just as we'd be getting up in the morning, Leonard Brooker would be coming home from his job at the bakery. And that was when, just after dawn, he'd put in his work-time for the Farm, chopping and stacking wood. *Zing, zing* was the sound of his ax in the crisp air. The wood was for everyone, through the long hush of winter. We'd look out over the snow or the misty purple-vetched meadow and see Leonard Brooker—far off to the east, his ax flashing up and down in the lavender light.

But none of this do I mention to Ivy either. As my mother reminded me this morning, "How we conduct our lives out here is nobody's business but our own." That's another thing she liked to say. I'd heard it a million times.

When my hair comes out of the curlers, Ivy makes me stand up and bend at the waist. Then she brushes my hair straight down toward the floor. "Wait now. Don't move," she says. "I've got to spritz it."

The spritz is cold on my neck, and the hair over my face surprises me with its sweet smell.

Ivy pats it like the back of a dog. "Okay. There."

I straighten up and feel the blood drain out of my skull. What I see in the mirror is a girl who resembles me: the same nose, wide at the bottom; the thin, pursed lips. I shake the mysterious spirals of hair.

"Not bad." Ivy pushes a few brown curls up over my ear and aims a spray at them. "You look at least sixteen." She feathers out the curls with her fingers and sprays again.

"And a good height on this hair," she's saying, but to herself now, since I, the old Marnie, am busy watching the new Marnie in the mirror nod, shut her Iced Peach lips, turn her apricot cheek to one side. This Marnie is confident. Her hair glistens, floats around her—more flattering to this girl than it was to the former one.

With the radio playing by the sink, Ivy holds the curling wand close to her mouth and sings "Love me two time, gal." Her eyes close. "One time for tomorrow, one time for today." Her cheering fans of canisters spray a perfumed mist around us.

Pauline, the woman who cuts hair at the Farm, has a pair of clippers—grass clippers with long steel blades—hanging off her porch beam. This is supposed to be funny. It's her business sign. A crystal windchime dangles from one of the blades. I used to believe this construction held some secret meaning—a snip and a resounding tinkle of the universe—but I don't think that now. Over the years the clipper blades have rusted orange. Sometimes with the other girls, the ones my mother calls my shadows, we take turns in Pauline's tire swing, watching the boys get their trims on her porch. She lifts a fringe of hair off their foreheads and swicks it off with her real scissors, a tiny silver pair. The boys like their hair short, very short, like Mr. Odeen's. "A real gentleman doesn't shove in line like that," he says to the boys in my class who'll be in his next year and then, no doubt, transformed. Mr. Odeen wears navy pants with pleats. His blond hair is trimmed high over his ears and the top combed straight back. His glasses are small, half-round discs he sometimes looks over the tops of, past our faces, past our giggles and shrieks, and out into the blowing maples. "Gentlemen," he calls into the throng at recess, "let's get control of ourselves."

The younger boys from the Farm are at the other end of the world from Mr. Odeen. They wiggle in Pauline's chair. She bends over them, her own hair sheared short and combed back as neatly as theirs. Her new toddler, which my mother says she found in the woods in Idaho, sleeps in my old dilapidated stroller. From the tire swing, we watch the boys. I'm the oldest girl, so it's my job to see that the small fry get pushed, high and hard, the way they like it. Especially that little one, Erin. She's four and has yet to say a single word. "Those girls—they're Marnie's lemmings," I heard Sonny tell my mother once. "They'd follow her off the edge of a cliff." Which is why, my mother says, I've got to stay sweet. Often from the tire swing we'll see—off by the log piles—a couple of boys making last-minute alterations to the spacecraft. We'll hear a deep bass bang. I push the girls. Sweetly, but not too sweetly. Little Erin puts her head back. Her mouth drops open. Though she won't say anything, maybe never even a single word, she takes in the loud craziness of the world. Like it's nothing.

The song stops and Ivy puts the electric curling wand in my hands. "Okay, now how 'bout me?"

I touch Ivy's hair, thick and cold. I scoop and gather it

up as if it's flying in the air above the trampoline again, and it feels as if I've plunged my hands into black icy water.

*   *   *

Stoney is the name of the boy we'd been watching squirm in Pauline's chair last week. My mother has asked me a thousand times why he's named that. Why? *Why?* Her voice accusatory. "How should I know?" Anyway, it's only one of his names. Brooker calls him Corporal Stoney.

I don't know, I keep repeating. What the boys say, what they do—it's not my business. I accept that. When Stoney was done with his haircut, he walked with me down Canyon Road. We watched the little girls slip back inside their houses. Then I showed him the animal graves we'd been making these last few weeks near the creek. I said, This is a possum; this is a cat—just its skull, since a cougar ate the rest. We're not afraid to touch dead bodies, I told him. But I didn't say how we get them all cozy down there, in their deathbeds, how we'd learned to stare right back at the rigor mortis. I didn't tell him that the more we do this, the more we steel ourselves against the same bad fate. We pat the dirt mounds flat.

When the moon came up, which must have been his signal, Stoney asked, "Can I kiss you once?" But he didn't. He kissed me twice. The first one was a miss, a do-over. His lips landed off-center on mine. We tried again, and I lifted my hands and touched his arms above the elbows.

Afterwards, he'd stepped back, looked at me. Over his ears was a pure whiteness where his hair had just disappeared.

"All right," he said, "that's good." I let my hands fall back to my sides. I pointed to the grave of a black snake, the grave of a squirrel. The girls and I, we know everything that's out there.

And farther off, behind the toppling beehive boxes, is Lila. A real person we all knew. Once, when I was a kid, she helped me make a doll, a Mr. Monkey, its red mouth the heel of a gray sock. She sewed on gold buttons for eyes. Last November she went down into an actual grave, dug all day by six men in the rain. Auntie Lila, we used to call her. I'd seen her, I told my mother, seen her only one year ago, in a May like this one, with lots of rain. It was just past dark and she and her boyfriend Wayne were standing by the creek, naked, all parts of them touching everywhere, standing with their heads back, their faces lifted to that cold drizzle. Yes, my mother said, it's all right, sweetie, they were just loving each other. The grass is cold after dark in a rain like that. Grownups on the Farm have a word they say about their lives. *Anarchy.* We can say it back to them. Tiny syllables like a mouth full of gravel. It's a hard word to work your mind around, but we're getting the idea. A rain can be warm on the cold grass, the dirt steaming when you slice into it.

Farther down the creek, hidden from plain sight by the high wood piles, is Brooker's house, where he lives with a man we all believe is crazy although we're not supposed to say so. When I play with the girls, which is more like baby-sitting in my mind, I watch for the old man, his reddish-blond beard pointed like a billy goat's, to step out of the Quonset. Wade Brooker's mother, we've heard, didn't last a year out here at the Farm. She left her infant space-captain son and hitched a ride to California.

The last time anyone saw Leonard Brooker close up was back in the fall at a residents' meeting. His red eyebrows thick—almost one eyebrow—over his nose, stern-faced, he'd stomped across the meadow in his green rubber boots and gone inside the lodge with the other grownups. Stoney and the boys came and stood outside the open windows. Inside, the old man was making a speech. He said there were signs, increasingly frequent signs, that the axes of the world were shifting. The off-kilter poles were triggering more earthquakes. Unrestrainable floods and droughts were about to strike, and D-day, the really big one, was on its way.

"So all right then, any other new business?" someone asked, but Leonard Brooker went on, warning the grownups about the skewed jet stream, a new ice age bearing down.

Outside the lodge, we glanced at one another, then stared at our feet. Suddenly Leonard Brooker came stomping out, past us, and headed back across the meadow. Inside, the grownups began talking, arguing really, about another matter: what to do with any dead one of us, which we—all of us standing outside by the windows—didn't have any idea meant our Auntie Lila.

"Where's Wade?" someone whispered. And then Stoney flung his arm out. He pointed: there was Brooker with a can of spray paint turning the propane tank blue.

*   *   *

The green hands on Ivy's clock creep together toward midnight. In her bed, she fans my hair out on a silky pink pillowcase. "All right, you be Brooker for a minute and I'll show you. I'll show you how it's done." Ivy leans her face close to me. Her sweet-smelling, dark hair brushes my cheek. "Just. Like. This." She puts her lips on mine.

My eyes are open, but Ivy's are closed. She's off in a long-gone dream of Brooker in which some entirely other version of me plays the starring role. She snuggles closer and presses harder against my mouth.

My hand pats her shoulder. I've done this kissing thing before so I'm less susceptible. And besides, I know how it's supposed to go.

If anyone believed Captain Brooker's recent interstellar flight lectures, they'd conclude that the spacecraft is nearly complete. It's bound for another galaxy. Getting spruced up, fitted out. Polished. Armed. Brooker has been busy, as he's told his crew, getting his brain into a direct interface with the onboard computer system. "It's thought-to-missile accuracy we're after," he says.

Gently, sweetly, I push Ivy away. "Quit it, Ivy."

"All right, you be me then, and I'll be Brooker." She lies on her side and smiles at me happily. "Okay, Marnie?"

"No." I cross my arms on my chest. "This is stupid."

Ivy flops onto her back, sighs heavily.

"He'll never love you in a million years," I say and pull the covers up to my chin. It's such a pressure on my patience to be sweet all the time. I hear Ivy let go two tiny sobs. The

Wade Brooker I know sits half in and half out of an absurd spacecraft. A tight ship, he calls it. The Ridiculous: painted cosmic blue. *Maximum warp*, he shouts into the summer twilight across a field of potatoes and leeks. Two aeronautical gentlemen in black baseball caps turn wrenches, adjust the screws for a vertical take-off. A test run. Charting the propulsion trajectory.

What Brooker knows about is the grand exit. To slip away from the very world the formerly sobbing but now sleeping Ivy wants so badly to enter. A minute ago she'd pressed her lips against the bare edge of it, and now she's closed her eyes and dropped off into the swirling thick of it. But Brooker, Brooker is leaving. The launch pad fogged by exhaust. He's going. He's gone.

THE LAND OF ANARCHY

(Sonny)

Since it seemed that the animals, at least for the time being, had quit dying, the five little girls were making ready to bury one of themselves. They'd laid out Erin, the youngest, in the middle of Sonny's gravel driveway and were sticking flowers up and down the length of her. Weeds, really. Dandelions and arrowleaf balsam root. The girls crossed, then recrossed Erin's arms over her chest and poked a few droopy larkspur in her short blond hair.

Watching from the back window over her sink, Sonny frowned but went on sharpening a pair of hoof trimmers, whisking the blades against a pumice stone in preparation for her work in the sheep shed. So far, like the other adults at Curtain Creek Farm, she'd managed to shrug her shoulders about the girls' funerals—for a possum, two wild barn kittens, a run-over garter snake, and who knew what else. But Sonny's nonchalance took some effort. When, among her neighbors, the subject of the children's death rituals came up, she offered a pinched smile and a gentle roll of her eyes. But inside she felt a tightening. She'd watched these girls grow up.

All through April, as they'd crunched the stiff limbs of animal carcasses into empty cereal boxes, they'd held intense discussions, which Sonny had overheard, about the progress of underground decay. And now this. This pretend-burial of that odd little Erin, the child who'd only recently come to them, to their protection at the Farm. Lice-infested and stony-eyed, the girl howled a wild feline screech if any stranger, any adult, touched her.

Sonny set down the trimmers and dialed Alison's number. "I think you should see what these kids are up to," she said. "If you're not too busy."

"What—another smushed critter in a Wheaties box?"

Sonny took off her glasses and wiped them on her shirt tail. She thought she heard Alison let out a deep sigh, although maybe it was simply an exhaling of cigarette smoke. Alison was the only one at the Farm who smoked, rolling a foul black tobacco inside bright yellow papers, a thing she did smugly, with a studied flourish and finesse.

"No," Sonny said, putting her glasses back on. "It seems we've entered a new phase." She couldn't make herself turn from the window. With those blue flowers in her small fists, the designated dead child did look lovely, decorated like a medieval corpse. She did, in fact, appear dead. Any stranger turning just then into Sonny's driveway would have thought so. And it crossed her mind that here was yet another reason for outsiders to think the Curtain Creek residents were nutcases. Members of some crazy death cult. The truth be told, they were members of nothing. All that held them together was their singularity. Occasionally people paired off for a while, but that was only, as her own ex-part-ner Reuben would have said, a matter of physiology. The body's willfulness.

The death business with the five little girls had been bad before, but not this bad. First, after they'd marched up her driveway—the oldest girl Marnie always in front carrying the battered box—they'd hold a little funeral right there in the gravel, then head off across the sheep pasture. For their ceme-tery they'd commandeered a green strip of land between the fencing and the creek. As best they could, the girls dug with hand trowels in ground that was still hard and icy, so that often a box's bright colors showed through after it was in the ground. For gravemarkers, the girls had scavenged an old bed-spring, a rusted-out bucket on a stick, a cracked ceramic light socket, a blue glass telephone insulator.

But none of that was what troubled Sonny. Not the digging. Not the junky array of gravemarkers. Or even the use of her driveway for the ceremonies. She'd hear the girls singing—usually a kid's song they'd learned in the Township School, but sung slowly, like a chant. "A tis-ket. A tas-ket. A green and yel-low bas-ket." The girls circled a box, pitched weeds at it. Inside was some road-kill the thawing snows had laid bare. Now, mid-May, still seeing the girls coming down Canyon Road, led by Marnie, and with the little blond Carrie banging on her coffee can, Sonny was sure she knew how it had all begun. This was what she needed to speak with Alison, Marnie's mother, about.

Outside, the dogs barked loudly, then ran down Sonny's driveway, past the girls, past the corral—no doubt in pursuit of a rabbit. The half-coyote, the one everyone called Big Dog, led the way. The girls paid the dogs no attention. Squatting in the gravel around Erin, they carefully picked out pebbles and made a buttonlike row of them up her yellow sweatshirt. A glass insulator over the barn door caught the afternoon sunlight and refracted a blue line across the dead girl's chest. Sonny shook her head.

Those insulators. Ten years ago the Farm had come into possession of a couple thousand of them when Reuben's father had died. Sonny was living with Reuben then, out past Canyon Road's dead-end, where Reuben still lived, alone now, in that half cave, half lean-to house with its dank dirt floors. All Reuben had wanted from his family home were those insulators. But he wouldn't, he said, set foot in Latah again. That town was everything, he'd told her, every god-damned thing in the regimented world he'd walked away from. And no way was he going back. Not to his mother's funeral or, nine months later, to his father's.

Reuben asked our neighbors Rollie, Scooter, and Don to go for him. He'd written detailed directions to the house, through miles of the Palouse's rolling wheat fields. *Turn left at the stand of red willows. Veer right as you pass the hog farm.* His father had worked the first half of his life for the phone company, stringing line—before he'd turned holy, as Reuben had told Sonny, before he'd taken to thumping Bibles as instructed by some burning bush.

Over the years, those insulators had become a kind of trademark for the Farm's shelters. Blue glass adorned roof peaks and garden fence posts. This past fall, when their neighbor Lila had died, someone had fused a dozen insulators into a two-foot-high marker for her grave. Lila's was the first real grave. And although Sonny had gone along with everyone then, lately she'd come to regret her acquiescence about letting the children attend the graveside ceremony. What the children had seen on that rainy November day— twenty-eight grownups weeping together around a gaping, muddy hole—wasn't a picture easily erased from a young mind. The box went down, and the volume of sobbing came up.

Calling Sonny's name once, Alison opened the door and held out a plastic bucket of flowers—white lilacs, blue columbine, and two dark purple irises. "Picked this morning," she said and set them on Sonny's chipped Formica table.

"Thanks." Sonny smiled at the flowers. "I love that lilac smell."

Alison nodded and walked straight to Sonny's back window. She had a yellow cigarette stuck behind her ear. "Cripes" was all she said when she leaned toward the glass. The auburn braids that hung halfway down her back swished when she turned toward Sonny. "Sometimes I think even TV's crap would be better than this crap."

"This is exactly what comes of exposing kids to those barbaric rituals." Sonny had let out the words in exactly the same caustic tone she'd been using in her mind. But aloud, they sounded wrong: wooden and mean. She stepped to the window and stood next to Alison. She tried to start over. "Our children have no . . . no context for stuff like that." Outside, the four older girls stood holding hands around Erin, who still lay in the gravel.

Alison jerked her head sideways. "You don't *have* any children, Sonny."

"Still," Sonny muttered. "*Still . . .*"

Alison had turned her gaze back to the window, but far past the girls, off into the distant trees. Then it dawned on Sonny what Alison must be looking for. Off and on for the last month, a cougar had been spotted among those cotton-woods at the base of the rock wall. Sonny had seen it herself. She'd even gotten out the field glasses just to be sure it wasn't simply a big yellow barn cat. But no barn cat had a tail like that: long and golden, dipping down along the ground, then curling back up. Clearly Alison was more worried about that cougar leaping out and lunging at a child, picking off, say, that bossy, skinny brunette, her own daughter Marnie, than she was about rituals.

"I guess I think of *all* the kids out here as mine." Sonny picked up the hoof trimmers and eyed along their newly honed blades.

"I know you do." Alison turned to her. "I'm sorry. This time next month they'll be into horseshoes or soccer, or—who knows?—origami." She crossed her arms. "Don't stress on this, Sonny. There are bigger things in the world to stress on."

"It's that little one I worry about. What's going through *her* head?" Erin hadn't been with them quite a year yet, and at four years old, she'd only learned to understand maybe ten words. Her foster parents, Carl and Dana, were giving her a home—for now, they said, but maybe for good. Dana was a social worker three days a week in Cusick, and she'd been the one on duty when the sheriff phoned.

In a frigid basement, the police had found Erin in a black dog collar chained to the leg of an old steel laundry sink. The girl's hair was so filthy and matted that Dana had to help a nurse cut it off, in big foul hunks, close to her scalp. The mother was an "end-of-the-road mainliner," which, Dana had explained, touching her own arms, meant the woman had used up every decent vein in her body.

"What are you fixing to do with *that*?" Alison nodded at the trimmers. "It looks lethal."

"Just give the sheep's hooves a little snip-snip-snip. This time of year I try to do a few every afternoon."

Alison took a step toward the door. "I could give you a hand if you want."

"Sure." Sonny bent and sniffed the lilacs as she passed them. "Lovely," she said, then nudged her glasses back in place.

When Sonny and Alison stepped outside, they saw the girls walking in long solemn strides across the pasture. Two of them, Jess and Kiki, were pulling Erin behind them by the ends of what, Sonny could now see, was a gray bath towel she'd been lying on all along. The procession left a flattened green swath in its wake.

Sonny held the barn door open. "We'll just do two or three," she told Alison. "Four, tops."

Alison hesitated. She stared off toward the granite rocks of the canyon wall. No one on the Farm could agree on what to do about that cougar. No one had a gun, at least not that anyone would admit to. It was their one rule: no violence. Dana and Carl had suggested calling the Department of Fish and Wildlife. They'd bring in a trap or maybe tranquilizer darts. But that idea was quickly vetoed with reminders of everyone's long-standing distaste for government people poking around. Pretty soon there'd be building inspectors and snoops from the Department of Agriculture.

"Well, if anyone should be worried," Sonny'd said at the last meeting, "I should. But I'm not. No cougar wants to trouble himself tangling with a whole pack of dogs. With one or two, maybe. The dogs do their jobs. Like all of us."

"The dogs can't be everywhere at once, Sonny," Dana had said. She wore little round wire-rimmed glasses these days, and her hair had been permed by someone in town so it wound around her head in soft curls. She'd come to resemble, Sonny supposed, a real professional woman. "A cougar wouldn't think twice about munching up some of our pups," Dana went on—ignorantly, Sonny thought. But after that meeting, each night she'd double-checked that the sheep were shut securely inside the barn.

Alison, still gazing toward the creek, touched Sonny's arm. "You don't suppose they're going to try to put that little Erin in the *dirt*, do you?"

Sonny smiled and shrugged, determined now to return to her original pose of calm apathy. Seeing that the child was on a towel had relieved her. *Our* children, she thought again. Everyone called them *ours*. The way they called the sheep *ours*, even though Sonny was clearly their caretaker. Just seeing the children step off the bus in the afternoons made her happy. They leapt down the big steps into the sunlight and dust of Canyon Road, and the first thing the kids did—in the late spring or early fall—was to take off their shoes. Sonny loved that: the way they shucked themselves loose from rules, the petty regulations that had held them all day.

Watching them, Sonny sometimes recalled her old fantasy: that one of those children would run through *her* door, sit down at the red table, and ask for a slice of home-made apricot bread. But even the subtlest suggestion of parenthood used to make Reuben's face tighten. During their five years together, he'd kept a white bowl of condoms on the floor by their mattress. Sonny, he'd say, children need a firm hand. And that's not us, *is* it? Anarchy is hard enough on adults.

In the barn as Sonny caught the first ewe, she realized she was showing off for Alison, but she couldn't help herself. The old ewe had sauntered lazily up to her, then stood waiting for Sonny to scratch her rump, which she did. Next Sonny leaned over the sheep as if to whisper a secret, then in one quick motion grabbed both front legs and jerked the sheep upwards, then back onto its rump.

Alison laughed. "She looks like she's just waiting for a cup of tea."

Sonny demonstrated. "All right, let her lean back against you like this. With all four feet are off the ground, they're totally discombobulated. They don't know *where* they are."

Alison stepped in behind Sonny and put her arms around the sheep. Sonny moved in front, knelt down, and began trimming the flaky edge of a hoof. With the blade tip she picked caked dirt from the hoof's crevice.

Sonny thought Alison looked tired, her face drawn, lined. Alison was single-handedly raising Marnie, a smart child, as everyone knew, but a headstrong one. The consensus around the Farm was that she took after her father—a man who'd never lived among them. He had a tidy red brick house in Spokane, and he came up once a month for a weekend, unloading from his bright green mini-van all sorts of items that raised eyebrows along Canyon Road: bags of gourmet potato chips, frozen steaks, a cordovan leather briefcase, and always that little portable television. No one could imagine what sort of reception he'd get out here where there wasn't a single antenna.

The sheep raised her head and baahed, and Alison, letting out a low-pitched wobbly note, mimicked her. The action in the barn soon drew an audience: a circle of a dozen ewes gathered to watch the trimming.

Sonny worked quickly. The sound of the metal blades snapping at the thick amber hooves was loud in the barn's quiet.

Alison looked around at Sonny from behind the sheep's neck. "This one's very fat."

"Very pregnant. Twins, probably. She's always the last to lamb. You can let her up now." The sheep got its footing and ran bleating to the curious onlookers.

Just then another sound—sharper and less familiar— rose above the sheep's cries. The girls. Screaming. Sonny dropped the trimmers.

Alison turned and ran for the door. Sonny, right behind her, slammed it closed. Three of the girls—Marnie, Jess, and Kiki—were racing across the pasture toward the barn.

"The cougar! the cougar!" Marnie was shouting. Jess and Kiki, wide-eyed, their arms flailing, stumbled through the tall grass.

"Where?" Alison caught Marnie's shoulder. "*Where?*"

Marnie raised her right arm and pointed back toward the canyon cliffs.

"Hey, you two! Carrie, Erin—get over here right now," Alison shouted at the two girls who were still standing by the creek, fifty yards away.

"Hurry!" Sonny called, realizing her own voice had none of the force Alison's had. Sonny glanced at Marnie. "Are you sure? I can't see him."

Alison knelt and pulled the three girls into her arms.

"Look, Sonny"—she jerked her head— "is that him? There, beside that red rock."

"That's him. That's him," Marnie said, her face buried in her mother's shoulder.

Sonny squinted, pressed the bridge of her glasses tighter to her nose, and took a step forward past the huddle of the others. All she could see was Erin trying to twist her arm out of Carrie's grasp.

Marnie jerked her head up. "No. Don't go out there, Sonny. Don't. Erin will just run away. She'll see you and she'll run. She's crazy."

Sonny stared hard at the jagged granite across the creek from the girls. Then she saw the cougar. His huge yellow head rose up from the grass below the rocks. He stared in her direction.

"You three kids, go on back to the barn," Sonny said softly, not turning but keeping her eyes on Carrie and Erin, who were still out there. "Let me and Alison handle this." She reached behind her back for Alison.

But there was no sound of movement behind her. Clearly Marnie, Jess, and Kiki were waiting for Alison's okay.

"Come on," Sonny said. "He'll just go the other way when he sees us." She felt Alison's hand then, still warm and greasy from the sheep.

Tugging on Sonny's hand, Alison pulled herself up. "He *sees* us, for Christ's sake, Sonny. He's enormous." She dropped Sonny's hand.

"Cougars don't attack unless they're riled." Sonny kept her voice calm, her eyes straight ahead.

The cat's thick tail swished. He stood just across the water from the girls and ten yards downstream. He lowered his head and raised it again, and as he did, a scream echoed across the field. But the cat's mouth, Sonny saw, was closed. It was Carrie who'd screamed. She'd let go of Erin's arm and taken a step back.

"*No.* Carrie. Stay put." Sonny began moving in long strides toward the two girls. "Stay where you are."

Then Carrie grabbed the hem of Erin's yellow sweatshirt and pulled. But Erin wouldn't budge.

Sonny, keeping the two little girls and the huge cat as the end points of her vision, kept trudging through the high pasture grass. Obviously Erin still hadn't seen Sonny, although the cougar, slowly lowering his head on his side of the creek, followed her progress with an unwavering gaze.

Then from nowhere, Reuben's tanned face loomed up suddenly in her mind. His dark eyes narrowed, he held her in as steely and steady a gaze as the cougar's. Slowly his head nodded down. The mirage of Reuben at that moment made her blink as she ran through the grass. In just that same unexpected way, the actual flesh-and-blood man himself occasionally visited her. There'd be his two quick thumps on her door, and in he'd step, sometimes not uttering a word, as if ashamed to need her still, after all this time. And the way he took her, gently, in his arms, smelling her hair. He'd press his lips against her neck, breathing her in. He'd been sent out in the middle of the night by his body alone. These days, the white bowl beside her bed held only a candle. No more small squares of cellophane. No more of that little rattling in the dark. Nothing, since both of them knew it was too late now for that.

Ten feet from Erin and Carrie, Sonny stopped. As her hands fell against her thighs, she could hear herself breathing—so loudly she was sure Erin would hear too, would turn, see her, and put her tiny hands over her face the way she did. But instead, Erin was mimicking the cougar: lowering her head slowly down, then hesitantly up.

What happened next, Sonny would, as the years passed, come to believe had occurred more in a dream than right there in the pasture. The cougar took two steps back, his sleek golden flanks almost pressed to the gray granite. Thinking he was about to leap forward, Sonny drew a breath and opened her mouth to shout, formed the *air* of Erin's name, but did not let it out—because then, just then, the cat swung away and loped off along his side of the creek.

Still watching him move away, Erin turned her head, and when she did, Sonny saw her face. She was smiling a soft lazy grin as if a puppet show had just been performed for her and had mildly amused her.

But in the next moment Erin caught sight of Sonny, and her grin vanished. Her face went hard and fierce. She put her hands over her eyes. Then she turned back the way she'd been before, facing the canyon wall.

"Come on, Erin. You know me. I'm Sonny. The sheep lady. Time to go home. Come on now."

Carrie ran to Sonny then, but Erin continued standing with her hands pressed against her face. Sonny put a hand on Carrie's head and glanced downstream. The cougar was gone.

"It's no use, Sonny," Marnie said, suddenly coming up with the others behind her. "Erin thinks if she can't see you, you aren't there."

Alison put her arm around Sonny's waist. "Cripes, I thought that cat was going to jump, didn't you?"

Sonny nodded. They stood huddled together. She felt her heart still pounding, drumming in her ears.

Then Marnie stepped past Sonny and went to Erin. Lightly she touched Erin's back and pointed to the gray towel.

Alison took the yellow cigarette from behind her ear, lit it, and inhaled deeply. As she and Sonny watched, Erin lay down on the towel and crossed her arms over her chest. Carrie picked up the coffee-can drum, and Jess and Kiki, taking the ends of the towel, slowly pulled Erin away from the creek. As she passed Sonny's and Alison's legs, Erin covered her face again. The few blue flowers still left in her hair had wilted, so it seemed she had only twigs sprouting from her skull.

Over the next few weeks Sonny kept dreaming the same dream: she discovers her sheep, all dead, lying in heaps around the corral. In the dream she is sure of the killer's identity. A man with a red-handled knife. He has slit the sheep up their middles. Pools of blood stain their white fleeces. But oddly, she's not angry with the man, whom she recognizes as Reuben. "It's all right," she tells him. Inside his dirt-floored house, the old gold lantern light surrounds them. "It's okay. I know it's just something you had to do." And then he pulls her to him, kissing her in his cool quick way, as if doing something sly. And what's strangest in the dream is his answer: "I knew you'd understand, Sonny. I knew one of these days you would."

In real life, Reuben had never used that knife for anything but cutting twine off hay bales, or, even after they were no longer living together, filleting a trout out on her back stoop. They'd never found a butchered sheep. Few at the Farm even ate red meat. They sold the ram lambs in town and tried not to think about the lambs' futures.

Two weeks after the cougar incident, as Sonny went out just before dawn to check on the sheep, she realized it was, yes, Memorial Day, a day that seemed to have existed long ago in another world. Back in that world, she'd gone with a set of her own foster parents—which set she could no longer remember—to a vast cemetery, almost a city unto itself. The foster parents said she was to help them "dress the graves." They gave her white peonies to set by the markers of their long-dead grandparents and an aunt who'd died as a young woman, Sonny remembered, of a hole in the heart.

All of that, Reuben used to say, was just a load of barbarity. And years ago, the way she'd loved him then, she'd believed what he said, believed the hurried, furious world they'd both abandoned was fraught with dogmas that enslaved their truest selves. And those selves could thrive, Reuben claimed, only out here in the pure light of hard labor with the munificent earth.

But that May morning she'd gone back inside the house and returned with the jar of flowers she'd brought home yesterday from Alison's. The little girls had gathered them—even Erin, who, still keeping her back to the grown-ups, had passed over her shoulder stems of coral bells and lupine. And Sonny, carefully not touching the child's fingers, had put them in the jar.

Now, while everyone else was still asleep, she'd head out through the fog and put the flowers on Lila's grave. No one would see her. No one would say she was following the edicts of a society thrashing in its death throes.

But as she stepped around the beehives toward Lila's blue glass gravemarker that was just catching the first purple light, she had to smile. Flowers were everywhere. A cluster of delicate pansies floating in a teacup. Lilacs and long white stems of spirea in a green wine bottle.

She set her jar among the others. Then she walked along the path the children had made to their own burial ground.

Last week when the final lamb had been born, Sonny had also found herself on this path in an early morning fog. She was carrying the old gray ewe's lamb, still wet, in her arms. It hadn't been twins this time but one huge and utterly dead gray lamb. She'd found the old ewe standing over it in the barn, kicking it gently, trying to make it move, bleat, suckle.

Holding the wet body against her chest, Sonny had grabbed a shovel and headed across the pasture. Behind her, her tiny house and the sheep barn twenty times its size were soon obscured by the fog. The farther she walked, the heavier the lamb felt in her arms. Its damp went into her, filled her ribs with its cold.

Sonny put the dead lamb on the ground and rubbed her arms with her hands to warm herself. When she looked down again, she realized she was standing in the children's graveyard. She was surprised by all they'd done. A dozen small rectangular burial plots had each been outlined with shiny mica-flecked creek stones. Tin cans, stuffed with weeds, dotted the graves. Atop four stumps, blue telephone insulators marked the cemetery's four corners.

The bottom of a rusty bucket, upside-down on a stick, had been painted with a face. Not a smiling one. Nor a frowning one. Just two black eyes, a nose, and a straight black line for a mouth. An ancient face staring down the roiling clouds all day.

A few yards past the last gravemarker—a bed spring with a doll's rubber head on top—she sank the shovel in the ground and began digging. Gradually the fog rolled back. The pasture greened up in the light.

As Sonny dug, she watched for the cougar. It wasn't that she was afraid of him, but simply that he'd come to inhabit—now and probably forever—that spot across the creek, where his long yellow body had suddenly turned and the thick tail flashed.

The dead need their place among the living. The children had figured it out. They had put themselves in charge of it, coming up the road singing Mother Goose dirges, carrying dandelions and red hand trowels. Their neat rock-lined graves formed a maze along the creek. They knew how the winter ice stirs the black cauldron of ants and maggots through the fur and the flesh. Here, the dead creatures in their cereal boxes could cook into a dark stew.

Sonny stabbed into the ground and lifted the dirt. She was now a servant in this court. She lowered the lamb into the hole and curled him snugly into himself, letting her palm linger on his soft cool mouth. The lamb wasn't the only lamb she'd ever lost, but it was the only one she'd ever buried. She pressed him into his place in the earth by the rock and the water.

MAKING HEADWAY

(Roxanne)

The fat black electrical cable that ran out the back of the Frito Lay truck looked like a tail. It bisected a field of cheat-grass, then rose sharply and inserted itself into a silver box halfway up a thirty-foot telephone pole. The webmaster himself had supervised the hookup. He knew what every one of the wires did, the white, plastic-coated ones and the copper ones—the mega-rams that each would soon be pumping out to his truck.

Sitting on her nest atop the pole, the old osprey let us know she wasn't happy about the hookup. "Yeek, yeek," she screeched at the telephone company men working below. We'd had the phone lines in at the Farm for ten years, and for the last nine, she'd had her nest on that pole, each year adding a few more sticks—willy-nilly—so that now the nest was three feet wide. Early mornings and at dusk, she'd head east to the Pend Oreille River where the salmon got stalled, flailing spastically against Davis Dam.

A handful of us—we who'd been keenest on inviting Frito, the webmaster, to visit Curtain Creek and get us situated on the net—stayed a few yards back, watching, ankle-deep in the bristly weeds.

Frito combed his fingers through the dangling wires. "It's amazing that bird hasn't been fried to smithereens."

The osprey stood up then, poked her beak over the mess of sticks, and squawked down at Frito and the orange-overalled man from U. S. West.

"Don't talk so loud, you guys," Alison told the two men. "You're getting her all freaked out."

"She'll get over it, lady." The overalled man yanked the black cable, taking up its slack, which made it swish, pythonlike, in the grass.

The bird's gaze followed the black line toward Frito's truck, with its faded decals of blue, red, and yellow bags of chips—tipped over, spilling out.

"That bird was nuts to move up there in the first place," I told Alison.

"Yeah, but I'm used to her now, Roxanne. I love to look out my window and see those little bald baby heads, don't you?" She took one of her hand-rolled yellow cigarettes from her shirt pocket and lit it.

The osprey stood with gnarled talons crimped to the rim of her nest. When she shook her wings open, they made a snapping sound like clean sheets catching a wind.

I wasn't yet smitten by Frito, although maybe I should have seen that coming. His black shirt sleeves were rolled up,

his forearms sprinkled with freckles. Head down, he studied
the mystery of the wires, clearly far ahead of the phone company man's knowledge of digitized uploads and downlinks.

"Yeek, yeek," went the bird—guttural, raspy.

Frito smiled and looked up. "Take it easy, sweetheart,"
he said and flashed her the peace sign.

*　　*　　*

It hadn't been easy to get a webmaster to touch down for a
couple of months at Curtain Creek. First, there were the sep-
arate issues of *if* we wanted a place on the world wide web,
and then *why*. Or if *why*, then *if*.

Melody and Leigh, who'd lived at the Farm for thirty
years, were against it. They'd bring their hand carders to the
resident meetings and sit on the floor, working their way
through a bag of fleece. "World wide web—that's w-w-w,"
Melody told Leigh one night. "Get with the lingo, kiddo."

Another neighbor, Leonard Brooker, had stood up and
said it was no joking matter. We'd be contaminated by cyber-
space garbage. "Let there be no mistake," he said, his thin
pointy beard fluttering, "we're only dragging ourselves closer
to the world-wide backfire."

Carl rolled his eyes. "We need to get ourselves out
there," he said. He and his wife Dana had real jobs, in
town, and Dana said she'd seen on the net at work how
other communes were growing. "Which *we* have to do," she
said. "We *have* to."

Now that we'd begun dying were the unspoken words in

the air around us that night. *Now* that we had a graveyard. *Now* that our numbers were dwindling.

The arguments went round and round. Some said we had to try, first just *try* to imagine it. There'd be color photos of the sandals and blankets we made. Buyers could see what they were getting. See real people making real stuff.

But finally what it came down to wasn't the selling of our wares. It was about combating our fears. One night Alison turned to us, tossing one of her long braids over her shoulder, and asked, "Shouldn't we at least have a look? The world's wide web: what *is* that anyway? Shouldn't we see for ourselves? Otherwise, it's like we're scared—scared of what we don't even know."

"We god damn *know!*" Leonard Brooker stood up, spun sharply, and stalked out in his green rubber boots.

*   *   *

For the first three weeks of Frito's stay with us, he went around collecting "our lives"—in two or three paragraphs apiece. This information would be part of our homepage. "A link," he explained at his introductory potluck dinner in the lodge, and when he said that, Melody and Leigh nodded knowingly, going along with everything now. We were nearing the end of June, and soon they'd be walking up Canyon Road toward my place: to ask me to lend them a hand washing filthy, dung-caked fleeces. They'd have four big kettles of hot soapy water bubbling over a fire behind their domed house. In and out the wool would go. *Gently, gently, Roxanne,* they'd remind me a thousand times.

Every fall the blankets and ponchos that came off the weavery's looms traveled to bartering fairs up in Priest River, or across the state to Seattle's Pike Street Market. And part of that money, a big chunk of the Farm's collective savings, had brought Frito to us. In the last five years he'd created websites for forty intentional communities across the U.S. He had a good reputation. We'd checked. We'd made calls.

When Frito's black sneakers with holes over each big toe kicked open his truck's back door, he stepped out into the summer sunlight, his black sombrero at a slant on his head, the red cord dangling below his chin. Going door to door with his clipboard, he'd call into a house, "Hey, what'd'ya say? Ready to do your bio?"

Inside my house, he let his sombrero fall so it hung down his back. The red cord's wooden bead bobbed on his Adam's apple when he spoke. "Wow, what's the story on all these cacti?"

"They belonged to a friend. To Lila. I guess you could say I inherited them when she died."

"Good," he said. "That's good. Why don't I put that down?"

I stared at the wooden bead, then up into his dark, unflinching eyes. "Is that *interesting?*"

He smiled. "Well, let's hear what else you got."

I went on about my budding career as a Rolfer, a kind

of massage therapist with a mission. I told him I'd given Alison four, so far, of ten Rolfing sessions to help her quit smoking and reduce her stress. I dug in around her ears and nose. I'd trimmed my fingernails down to the quick to get in there good, under her nicotine-buzzed, sphincter-tight smoker's muscles.

For a few weeks I'd owned a portable massage table. Another neighbor, Geneva, had bought it for me, the deluxe model. I described it to Frito, how its three sets of legs folded down so it could take a heavy body on top of it, not to mention my own hard pressure bearing down. To be a good Rolfer meant first to see exactly how the body—as if it were a building—had lost its architectural integrity, how gravity and habit had set it slouching with head too far forward, or had made it hypererect, bowing backward. Then you had to maul your way in to pull those muscles out straight, unclog the nerves' pathways.

But like most *things*—store-bought and expensive—the massage table was gone in a month. *Abandoned* was the actual word my mind kept repeating to taunt me. An *abandoned* property.

I'd left it in the living room of a man's double-wide trailer—with him still on it—down the highway in Usk. I'd stepped out his door. I hadn't run. I wasn't afraid of him. Not exactly. I'd calmly started the Farm's pickup and headed back to Curtain Creek.

What had gone wrong—and this part I didn't mention to Frito—was my own fault. I'd gone around the parking lot of Faith Valley Presbyterian Church putting my Xeroxed fly-ers on car windshields. I'd been trying to integrate myself into a capitalist enterprise. Fast money. A predator whose prey is bound, one day, to turn on her.

The man's problems, he told me after I'd plunked open the table legs on his gold shag carpet, were sexual. But he doubted a slip of a girl such as myself could help him. He had trouble making his lady friend happy—if I knew what he meant.

"Not entirely," I'd said.

"Well, basically, I was wondering"—he turned on his side, facing me—"I mean I thought you might do something for me"—and he glanced between his legs—"down there. Just, you know, for therapy."

"Kee-rist. What did you *say?*" Alison wanted to know when I told her, which I should never have done.

"I just told him that kind of work was out of my realm."

"Presby-fucking-terians!" She'd stared at me, then shook her head. "Honestly, going to some strange guy's house like that in the first place: what *were* you thinking, Roxy?"

*   *   *

Last week Alison spent two afternoons planting pink double-poppies in front of my place—the bus house, everyone called it, although you could hardly see the yellow of the school bus anymore, not since I'd extended a sheet of corru-gated aluminum off the bus roof. I'd framed in tall screen windows beneath it to hold it up. The screens I'd found over in Colville, tossed out on a curb for garbage pickup.

Sitting inside my new screened-in porch, I'd pop a cold beer and watch the kids on their bikes racing the dogs up and down Canyon Road.

Lately Frito had been appearing at my screen door with gifts: a big candy bar wrapped in gold foil, a box of colored pencils, and a bracelet he'd made himself, a braid of purple, blue, and black wires from his dissected, obsolete computer cables. A lanyard of sorts. Someone in a Utah commune had shown him how. He said he was good with his hands.

"Obviously," I said. "You should put that in your *own* bio."

He looked out toward the road, where the dogs were a blur far ahead of the kids. "And just whose website would I be on, Roxanne?" He leaned toward me and touched the bracelet on my wrist.

The two paragraphs of my life mentioned my Farm-famous tortillas and then my Rolfing. It said my intense manipulation of connective tissue could relieve lumbar distress.

Some evenings after I'd made tortillas, Frito and I would take a walk, stopping to chat with neighbors about the spring crop of lambs or who'd caught what sort of fish in Waitts Lake. Later, we'd settle into lawn chairs outside his truck. We'd watch the sun bite off the tip of Cee Cee Ah Mountain, then gnaw its way down the other side.

The old lady osprey, her wings flashing with a barely audible swoosh-swoosh over our heads, flew back and forth to the river, on a mission to nab one of the hundreds of berserk salmon pitching themselves against the dam. Rumor had it a man's body was stuck in that wall—right where he'd fallen, sixty years ago, into the wet cement. Oldtimers claim that when the river's low, you can make out the outline of a leg and a boot, which, they say, is just the price of progress: whatever falls in its path gets paved over.

Back in her nest, the osprey would devour the fish, then retch it back up, parceling out meals into the three babies' mouths. The odds were that maybe one out of the three would survive. Kids from town liked to shoot at them. Eagles and other osprey raided the nests. Frito and I watched the mother take off again, catching an updraft through the canyon. Those mouths—their constant calling, their swirling, dancing openness—surely seemed the be-all and end-all of her days.

I told Frito a good Rolfer could change a person's entire look so that his own sister wouldn't recognize him. I touched his face. "Where your chin is long and angular here, we might realign your tendons, tighten these up, and give you a rounder, smoother look."

I stood behind him and worked one of his shoulders, then the other. I told him I'd tried for a while to get a few chiropractors to refer patients to me. But no one wanted to drive way out here to the Farm for Rolfing sessions. We were so far off the beaten path, it was a joke. And by the same token, I hated to go into town. All those traffic lights bugged me.

"They bug me too," he whispered. He was putty in my

hands then. I got in behind the muscles of his neck and kneaded them. That was where, clearly, he kept all his worries.

What I could do to his face was a kind of dream I lingered in each morning as I awoke, making improvements. I had to see it first in my mind's eye. I had to look hard. Then I could make it happen. Tighten up the sag above his Adam's apple. Stretch his cheek muscles up, slowly, and realign them more proportionally to his mouth. His smile could be more subtle, I thought, convey his essential whimsy.

"So, *so* long," I said about the tendons. His head rolled in my palms. He'd been keeping too much for too long to himself under that big black hat.

When, moments later, he pulled me down on his lap, I was dizzy. Dizzy and probably nuts to tell him no then. "No, I can't. I can't."

"Your husband's been in Alaska three years, Roxy." His voice was soft and low, breathed out slowly in my ear. He slipped his hand under my shirt.

I pulled his fingers away and kissed them. "Everyone here knows each other's business, don't they?" Then I kissed his chin and his cheeks where I'd rubbed the beginning of a new softer look into his face. I should take photos, I thought: a before and an after. The Frito face that was coming in clearer in my mind would take three or four months. It felt like a project. It gave my morning dreams some purpose. Barely awake, I'd feel my fingers dig in.

*   *   *

To balance the long, sweltering hours over cauldrons of boiling wool, there'd soon be swimming too. I couldn't seem to remember to tell Frito that should also be part of my bio: how I take the kids down the lily trail to the pond. In the water the kids are screaming banshees. At first we swim near the cattails where it's warmer. Then out I'll go, arm over arm, across the pond and back, turning up the muscle volume all along the length of myself.

Nor have I given Frito much of anything from my old life. What would I tell? My husband gone off to Alaska three years ago? To fish, he said, where there were still wild salmon in abundance. Or should I mention those dark mornings of my childhood? Reveille drowning out the roosters. I was four years old when my father came home from Guam, appalled that I still hadn't learned my table manners. He shouted at my mother: surely she hadn't been too busy to teach me to hold a fork properly. What had she got to do all day? He opened a newspaper and laid sheet after sheet of it on the floor. Then he put my plate of food and my silverware down there. "Sit, young lady," he said to me. My mother's face went white. She turned it toward the Army green cupboards. "Sit down there on the floor if you're going to eat like an animal."

*   *   *

The Farm's homepage was finished, Frito announced last night at the meeting. "And you're all in here, of course—*Residents*, the number-one link." There was a linked page about the garden too and our earth-friendly agriculture.

Potato bugs we swirled with horseradish—homegrown and hot—creamed in a blender and then daubed on the plants with a pastry brush. Frito downloaded the site on the lodge's computer. A dozen of us gathered around as a gold band opened down the screen's left side. Very classy, I thought. Then a color photograph of Curtain Creek Canyon itself appeared, a crimson sunset flooding it.

"Okay," he said and clicked on a gold-and-blue oval beneath the rosy canyon, "here's a link that tells about the weavery. Melody and Leigh, Sonny, and all you gorgeous spinning ladies. Excetera."

On the screen, Melody's head and then her spinning wheel came into view.

"Amazing," Leigh said.

Frito grinned. "And oh yes, there's information about your philosophy." He nodded to me. "Why don't you hit that link and read what it says, Roxanne?"

I tapped a blue oval called *Philosophy*. Then, raising my voice to be heard over the kids outside, I read a paragraph about our distrust of hierarchical authority. *"Residents seek to unhinder one another from the maximization of their human potential."*

"No shit." Melody turned and nodded to Leigh.

Outside, two boys were screaming "Fuckhead" at one another, each claiming the other to be a bigger one.

"I'm not done yet," I said, continuing. *"People can manage their own lives through cooperation, mutual respect, and creative intelligence."*

Standing behind me, Melody had begun reading that among our various anarchies were an eco-anarchist, a neo-paganist, a primitivist, an anarcho-syndicalist, a mutualist, an anarcha-feminist, and a practical anarchist. Everyone stared around the lodge at each other, trying to guess who went with what term. I glanced into the nodding faces, which seemed to radiate a calm acceptance that yes, we'd clearly left the safety of our enclave now. But it seemed all right. We'd done it. We'd zapped ourselves out into the grand shebang.

Alison smiled at me and stepped outside. She stood in the doorway and shouted at the children to put a lid on it. Then she lit a cigarette, and no sooner had the first tiny smoke cloud risen above her than the June breeze shredded it and blew it away. So many flowers to plant and so few weeks to do it. For hours at a time her arms and hands were in motion—a veritable flower-machine. Dirt and tobacco had turned her nails black. She had six more Rolfing sessions to go with me, but my overall prognosis of an end to her smoking wasn't good. Her heart wasn't in it.

Soon Frito would be leaving, bumping his truck out of the sticky grass that was already browning up in the long rainless days. He'd told me his life was a life he was tired of now: too many months on the road and not enough downtime. "And your canyon here, Roxanne, is starting to have a certain potent appeal. But I'm not much of an anarchist." He sighed. "The others, they wouldn't want me, would they?"

As if *I* knew the answer. I shook my head. It's what

we all do best. No and no and no. We turn, point our chins in another direction. It takes so long out here, I told him, so so long, to get to yes. We brush the sides of an answer. Talk some more. Give us a winter and a spring to decide. Maybe a summer too.

*   *   *

Once the snows came I didn't drive the Farm truck anywhere. Few of us did. We had all the food we needed, stewed and sealed and put up high on our shelves. Let the others think as they will that I'm lonesome on my own, and I am, sure, but that's the secret center of my happiness. I'm good at dark cold mornings. Joyful violins on the tape player, black turtle beans on the stove, the spinning wheel whirring. Afternoons: a few sit-ups to hard rock, skeining off the spun wool. The hours fly by. For days, not a single *no* to be said, but the whole life a kind of *yes* quietly proffered.

On the first warm day we dared to take the path to the water and wade in, I felt like a big bear emerging from my cave. The kids and I followed the mule deer's path across the meadow, where we had indeed often seen bears romping, hugging themselves, and rolling, turning their bellies to the sun. At the pond, a few boys would throw themselves into the water right away, while the girls watched their faces, gauging the cold.

Then in I'd go. I could get lost inside my body in the water. I'd thrust my arms forward—farther, harder. I'd imagine a man in Alaska walking out on a glacier in the frigid air.

He breathes it down deep into his lungs. It has made him forget my name. And no, it's not him I continue loving, but the love itself. The roar of that through me. That, I think— that, or nothing.

*   *   *

The woman who'd bought me the portable massage table was Geneva. She'd lived with us for many years, but now only occasionally visited on weekends. She'd struck it rich making lampshades out of homemade paper and willow twigs. Geneva had low back pain. Too much bending and stooping was *her* theory, and I'd nod. But I knew she was in love with a boy half her age, the son of our dear dead friend Lila, buried now behind the beehives.

I made Geneva bend at the waist. "Bad, bad, bad," I scolded her, then dug in around her spine where the connective tissue had indeed shortened up. I pulled and squeezed.

"Oow, that hurts, Roxy."

"A lot?"

"More than a little."

"Better lie down then. We need to resolve your torso and pelvis into a more supportive relationship."

I tried for Geneva. I really did. Over the ten weeks of her sessions with me, she gained an inch in height. Her butt and belly tucked in nicely. She was a grown woman, spooked by love, and we weren't talking about that. My guess was that her tension came from her mind's continual command to run away from the very love her heart had already embraced. Her torso was begging to stay put, but the rest of her wanted to get the hell out of town.

Still, I wasn't sure. People's faces . . . what they say . . . it's never one hundred percent what they mean. On the phone, that man from the church had seemed so kind, his voice unassuming. But obviously I hadn't heard him right. And when I recall him there on my table, I see now what I'd missed then. His hand, as he'd turned on his side and pushed his towel away, had been trembling.

All the way home I kept thinking about the bumper sticker on his shiny Honda, which I'd recognized from the church parking lot. *When the rapture occurs, this car will be driverless.* What did that *mean?* I could only imagine a red car speeding down Highway 2 with no one at the wheel.

*　　*　　*

A week after our website was completed, Frito and I were sitting out a thunderstorm in his truck. His computer screen was lit up with a list of what looked like codes—letters and numbers. Frito kept his left hand on my left shoulder and leaned over me, touching the screen with his right. "See, these are the sex pictures. Tons of them. Just click on any number."

I sat at his computer in his black vinyl swivel chair. It squeaked when I moved. "What's all this other stuff?" I pushed the mouse so the arrow pointed to a picture of a girl opening and closing her white-stockinged legs. *I've got what you want,* the caption read. *Come on inside.*

"No, don't click on *her*, Roxy. That's just junk.

Banners. Stupid ads." Frito stood bending down, his face close to mine. "I'll bet nobody ever Rolfs the Rolfer," he whispered. His fingers pressed in—nowhere near my neck's complicated musculature, but traveling down toward my shoulder blades.

A lightning bolt cracked, a brittle splitting far off over the Pend Oreille; then came a deeper rumbling closer by.

"Pick a number, any number. Who knows how long our power's going to hold?"

I clicked on one, and the box on the screen said *Open this link.*

Frito ran his hands down my arms and put his chin on top of my head. "We can stop if you don't like it," he said. "Nothing gross." He touched his mouth to my forehead as the first drops plunked against the truck roof. Columns of electronic equipment were stacked all around us. Racks of modems. Bright wires trailed down like vines from ceiling hooks.

When the first image finally appeared, it opened downward like an Egyptian scroll—the girl's mass of blond curls, then the surprised little O of her mouth. But then the girl stopped—halted, right below the neck, until slowly her breasts began to materialize as if just invented. A long red fingernail tapped at a nipple.

Frito knelt beside me. He put his hand on my thigh.

In the last third of the screen, as it gradually lightened, were not one but two penises inside the woman. I shook my head. "Nah, I don't think so."

"What?" He squeezed my leg. "What?"

"Is that even possible?" I nodded to the screen, where the two men were invisible but for their genitals.

"That's the combo front door/back door," he whispered. "See how much you can learn on the net, baby?" He kissed my arm that was stretched toward the mouse. "Try another one."

I did. Then another. Outside, the thunder cracked like huge tree limbs breaking off. The pictures unfurled. Shaved flesh. Oiled and pink. Sex toys I'd never seen—blue hoses, candles, cones. Everything pressing, digging down into what I couldn't imagine opening like that—with my own two hands helping—before a camera's zoomed-in eye.

Frito fumbled at my jeans zipper.

"Wait," I said. I couldn't look away from the screen's slow unfolding.

"You go ahead. Just watch, baby."

And as if from far off with the rain, I heard a zipper unzip.

The truck door was propped open, just a crack, where the cable ran out; the air inside was thick. Damp. Rain pelted against the truck's side panels, against those painted bags of munchies—spilled open with the droplets trickling through the chips and pretzels.

Then, *crack!* The lights flickered. Swells of flesh blinked purple, blinked crimson. A throbbing the sky responded to. A man's tongue flashed across a swath of smooth mauve flesh, and a hand, warm and caressing, dipped two fingers down. Someone saying, "Yeah, all right. It's all right."

With my head back in the squeaking chair, I closed my eyes and pictured the heavens zinged and zapped. All that power with nowhere to go but back in on itself. And in the intervening seconds of quiet, we heard the osprey. Flapping through a sky cross-hatched by sizzling skewers, her wings made a loud *thwock-thwock*. Then she screamed. It was a piercing shriek right overhead, as if she'd looked inside the truck, as if our nest were now, like hers, lidless.

The lights flickered, then quit. Another lightning crack boomed—close as our own breaths—and suddenly it no longer seemed the sky had shot it down, but rather that the meadow, reaching up beyond itself, had sucked it in.

BESIDE OURSELVES
(Jeannette)

The children shrieked and ran. They dashed through puddles, stampeding like spooked sheep. Their squeals of happiness sounded like cries of panic. The rain had started suddenly—in the middle of the race—and obviously no one in charge had a plan about how to stop a race like this once it had begun.

Jeannette stood with the mothers and fathers on the north side of Monroe Street, looking where they looked: north, up the hill, over which the hordes of children kept coming, cresting the top under a huge black cloud. Wave after wave, the children hurled themselves, squealing as they hit the downhill grade. They kicked up water and splashed the bystanders who stood under brightly patterned umbrellas of daisies or zebra stripes or yellow smiley faces. Flinging their arms wildly, the children in no way resembled real runners. They ran like children stricken, on the verge of seizure. But they were smiling. Dousing the wet world with more wet.

Coming out of the Dental Academy and slipping her denim jacket over her blue hygienist's uniform, Jeannette had stood dazed among the cheering crowds for a moment before she remembered the race. Junior Bloomsday, they called it. The cold rain stung her cheeks. The middle of April and already she'd have to worry about getting home; how easily Route 2 along the Pend Oreille River slicked over, flooded even. It didn't take much.

She walked east and turned the corner, threading her way through people rushing past, many wearing white garbage bags on their heads, clutched closed at the throat. A man shoved one in her face. "Here, missy, keep yourself dry." It was Mr. Dines from the pawn shop. She'd cleaned his teeth a few months ago, but now, out of that context and on *his* street, he didn't remember her. She shook her head and pressed on. She'd been wetter, she told herself—wetter and colder.

She ducked into the Parkade and took the elevator to the Brown Level. She pushed her hand into her right pocket and wound her fingers around the little packet of dental tools she'd "borrowed" from the school. She'd promised a couple of her neighbors at the Farm that she'd give them a cleaning and a polish. Some of the residents there hadn't seen a dentist in forty years.

The elevator doors dinged open, and there, leaning against Jeannette's truck, was the girl, Ann Marie. It took Jeannette a few seconds to recognize her: her head was shaved, and a purple-and-green snake had been tattooed on her skull.

The girl, with her arms behind her, was propped against the front grille, her legs crossed at the ankles. "I saw your truck," she said, not moving. "I thought maybe you'd be going in my direction."

"I doubt it. I'm going home." Jeannette sighed. She didn't have a single thing to say to the girl.

Ann Marie nodded. A peal of thunder boomed to the south and they both turned their heads.

"He's still in intensive care," Jeannette said. "In case you're wondering." She stepped to the driver's side and unlocked the truck door.

"I know. I called the hospital." A crack of lightning blasted. "If those little tykes don't get themselves drownded, they'll surely fry." Ann Marie glanced past the row of fenders toward the south, then walked around to the passenger side and stood by the door. "Okay, just let me off at the freeway exit."

"To do what?"

Ann Marie shrugged. "Whatever."

"Why don't I take you to the shelter?"

Slowly, as if in pain, Ann Marie dropped her forehead against the top of the truck door.

Jeannette opened her side and got in. Through the passenger window she saw the girl, her bright red rain slicker, her hand on the door handle. Jeannette leaned across and popped the lock.

"Your windshield wipers are for shit," Ann Marie said as they left the Parkade and turned onto Main.

The rain fell in sheets. "Buckle your seat belt. Please."

Jeannette realized she'd have to concentrate on the road. Kids, evidently escapees from the race, were fleeing the scene. Everyone dripped as they ran. Police sirens wailed behind them, and Jeannette kept glancing in her rearview mirror to see if she needed to pull over.

"Aren't you going to visit him? I mean now?"

"No. I can't. I'm not allowed."

Ann Marie turned and stared at her, which made the green face of the snake, arced around her right ear, seem to lurch to attention.

Jeannette had to force herself to look back at the road. "They've got an immediate-family-only policy on his room right now." She'd let the girl off where she wanted, in two more blocks, under the freeway overpass, where she'd be dry and among her pals, the other street kids. They skateboarded there. Just last month Officer Stuart Duncan, the man lying in Room 417 of Sacred Heart, had brought them a bundle of blankets and a bag of tuna sandwiches.

The Law is what the kids called him. "Don't fuck with The Law," a boy with a safety pin through his lip had shouted to her once as she'd waited in her truck while Stuart got them sundaes at McDonald's. At the time she hadn't known that that was their name for him, and she'd sat there wondering what crime they suspected her of committing.

She hadn't known about the name until last week, after he'd been shot in the head and given a "very bleak" prognosis, according to Stuart's mother. Mrs. Duncan spoke curtly on the phone to Jeannette, who was still, in her eyes, the unmet, unseen *girlfriend*, not the *fiancée*, since Jeannette and Stuart hadn't quite gotten around to letting his family know about their engagement. They kept waiting for the right moment. Jeannette inferred, though Stuart had never said, that his parents wouldn't take it well when they found out she'd been raised at a place like Curtain Creek Farm.

His mother told Jeannette some kids had called and shouted into the phone, without even an hello, "Is The Law going to live?" Stuart's mother thought the callers were accomplices of the shooter's, but the shooter, it turned out, was a boy from the north side. He'd aimed a gun out his brother's station-wagon window, just to see, he explained to the cops, just to see what would happen. The brother himself had turned the boy in, sobbing at the station, saying he hadn't known his brother *had* a gun or when exactly he'd become a lunatic.

"He's not even conscious," Jeannette said to Ann Marie. She pulled into a parking lot under the freeway. Seeing a Dumpster there, she was reminded that that was where Stuart had said he'd found the tuna sandwiches, frozen—on top of the Dumpster lid. Overhead, the rain and the traffic made a whirring hum—shrill and loud, or low and thunderous when a semi went by.

Ann Marie glanced around but made no move to get out. On weekdays the parking lot was packed with the cars of people who worked up the hill at hospitals or downtown in the banks and shops. But now it was mostly empty, just a few cars, and no teenagers, none of the usual crowd. One whole end had been cordoned off by a yellow fence—for the kids' skateboarding. Inside the fence were stacks of old tires, plywood ramps, a couple of lawnchairs, and the Dumpster. The area had been Stuart's idea, and yes, he told the parks commission, he'd patrol it himself and make sure the kids didn't panhandle, smoke weed, or fornicate right there in plain view.

"As if they don't have other, better places to do those things," he'd whispered to her that night after the voting went his way. His mouth had been cool against her neck, his breaths soft and quick.

Ann Marie put her head back against the truck seat as if she meant to take a short nap. "I'm sick of the dog track," she said finally, her eyes closed. "The track stinks when it rains."

"Yeah, I'll bet." Jeannette nodded. "Don't you have any juju to make this rain stop?"

"Like I told you before, I'm not with that anymore. I quit."

Jeannette put her head back too. "Just a joke." The girl was so young, still uncertain about irony, what to take seriously and what not from the adult world. Jeannette turned off the ignition and closed her eyes. Most of her anger at the girl was gone. Maybe all of it.

The rain and the traffic overhead made a steady racket. Since Stuart had been shot last week, in whatever small pauses she had from her dental school tests and lab reports, she'd found herself recalling a scene she'd witnessed last January: two large black men, their heads bent, each with a hand on one of Stuart's shoulders. She'd pulled open the back door of the Crosstown Church—just slightly—and stood watching them. She'd been late, very late, and when she saw them that way, praying in the white church kitchen, she was hesitant to step inside, to make a sound. Clearly they were in the midst of some transaction with the Lord.

From the top church step she heard the timbre of their voices but couldn't make out their words. A thin line of warmth, through the door's slim opening, ran down her face. She realized the empty chair on one side of the small table was meant for her. This was to be their prenuptial meeting with the two men who'd officiate at their wedding—not Stuart's family minister down in Tekoa, but these two men, Reverend Dave and Brother Earl, who ministered to the street kids.

She'd been late because she'd been driving around looking for the girl—this girl, Ann Marie—in a Spokane neighborhood, where the old dog track and the Hound's Tooth Bar, now boarded up with plywood, had stood. Behind the track itself—overgrown with icy skeleton weeds poking through the snow—was a row of crumbling dog kennels. And that's where the girl and her friends lived, Stuart had told her. Inside those dog huts, the police had found bedrolls and knapsacks. Doughnut boxes and syringes.

Some nights Stuart would lie awake, throw the covers off, then on, then off again, and get up to stand and stare out his bedroom window into the chartreuse glow of crime lights. When he was sleepless like that, Jeannette was sure it was the girl's fault, sure the girl meant to steer him into a labyrinth of dark alleys, where she alone was queen. His ulcer, the doctor said, was exacerbated. Jeannette cooked him mild broths: no onions, no garlic. The hole in his stomach—as she imagined it on the x-ray—was a burgeoning shadow. Day by day, millimeter by millimeter, it widened. As January's nights grew deeper and blacker, Stuart's breaths on the window appeared wider, whiter.

Ann Marie had shown Stuart and his partner, Mitch, a doll she'd made—an Officer Duncan doll, she called it. Mitch had grabbed the Polaroid out of the squad car and snapped the picture.

"This is so great," he told everyone in the substation later. "Priceless." He'd taped the photo of the girl and the doll to Stuart's locker. But Stuart yanked it down.

"All right, here she is then," Stuart said one night, and he'd handed the picture to Jeannette. "Just so you have some idea what I'm dealing with."

In the photograph, Ann Marie, with waist-length, straggly black hair, stood by the squad car, defiantly holding the doll with its tiny rag-head. Ann Marie had the whitest face Jeannette had ever seen. The doll, on the other hand, had no face per se, no lips or eyes. Two twigs penetrated its chest, one pearl-tipped hatpin pierced its head, and smaller pins were pushed into its groin, its neck, its thighs.

Stuart shook his head. "That doll's a joke." He took the picture and dropped it on top of potato skins and melon rinds in the kitchen trash.

"You're not worried then?" Jeannette watched his face,

his pinched smile. Paroled murderers knew his name. Pimps down by the Sunshine Tavern rhymed it with tortures, singing little jingles right to his face.

But Stuart, with his late-night stubble like a trail of black silt along his jaw, rolled his eyes. "In the grand scheme of what's out there, this equals zero. A big fat zero. Don't you get it?"

Later she'd stood with him at the window and they'd watched the lights downtown. Deserted by its bankers and brokers, who lived in the ridgetop suburbs, Stuart's city changed at night. Down at its depths, among flickering lights, where voodoo fires blazed near the dog track, a careful observer might even see it happen. *Transmogrification,* she thought, that word she'd learned in her one elective class, World Religions. Howling and giddy with hooch, the kids danced and swirled themselves into puffs of smoke that blew across the river.

In bed she'd pressed her thighs against Stuart's to warm him, thinking about how she might answer his question. He laid a cold hand on top of hers, and gradually his breathing slowed down. His fingers slipped away. I'm *trying,* she was saying to herself, I'm *trying* to get it.

And that's what she'd been thinking as she stood that day with a line of warmth coming at her through the church's back door. She was trying to *get it,* though at that moment the *it* seemed enormous: shrouded, unfathomable.

The rain rapped loudly against the truck window, and Jeannette sat up.

Rap, rap, rap went the sound again. "You two okay in there?"

She turned and saw a man's face outside her truck window. He moved back, and she saw his blue policeman's uniform under his plastic slicker. She rolled the window down an inch.

"Hey, don't I know you?" he said, leaning down again. "Stuart Duncan's girl, right?"

"Fiancée," Jeannette said.

"Oh"—he nodded solemnly and glanced across the seat—"I guess you've heard then. I'm sorry."

"Heard *what?*" She rolled her window down farther, hearing, as she did, the passenger door squeak open. She glanced to her right.

Ann Marie had already gotten out. "Listen," she shouted across the top of the truck, "we're not doing anything of interest to you here. All right?"

"Christ, not *you!*" he said. "Voodoo girl." The policeman straightened up.

"I've . . . quit . . . that!" Ann Marie's fists were clenched.

Jeannette jerked open her door and stepped out. She was standing right in front of him. "What *about* Stuart?" She felt out of breath as if she'd been running for a long time.

He kept his eyes on Ann Marie.

Jeannette watched her own hand go out. It yanked hard on the yellowed plastic of his slicker. "Tell me. Now."

"I'm sorry. I shouldn't have said anything. I thought, I

just figured . . ." He glanced at her face, then at the truck. "He passed away this morning."

"Fuck." Ann Marie slammed a fist down hard on the truck roof. The noise reverberated around them.

The officer took a step toward Jeannette, who was shaking her head at him slowly, from side to side.

Ann Marie came around the truck and stood next to her. "Go on now," she said to the cop. "Go nab yourself some jaywalkers."

"Just what sort of trouble are you up to?" He spoke quietly and directly to Ann Marie as if Jeannette wouldn't hear.

"She's with me," Jeannette said.

The policeman stood frowning at them for a moment, then turned and went back to his car. He sat behind the wheel, watching as Jeannette and Ann Marie got back in the truck. Jeannette watched him through the rearview mirror as he jotted something on a clipboard.

Jeannette felt her hands trembling on the wheel.

"Better let me drive," Ann Marie said when the cop had pulled away. "You're in no shape." She got out, slammed her door, and came around to Jeannette's side. "Scoot over," she said through the still-open window.

Jeannette turned to her. "Do you even have a license?"

"I can drive." She nodded to her old place across the seat. "Don't sweat it."

Jeannette slid over. "What if he's lying? Maybe we should call." She put her head back against the seat.

"Yeah, that's good. We'll call." Ann Marie backed them onto the road, and Jeannette watched the truck move out into the heavy rain and the afternoon traffic as if she weren't even inside it.

Ann Marie drove a few blocks to a Safeway and pulled in next to a phone booth. "What's the number? I'll call." She picked out a quarter from the change in the truck's ashtray.

"No, I'll do it."

On the phone the nurse told her she'd have to check. "Oh yes," the nurse said when she came back, "here you are. Jeannette Briggs. 'Girlfriend,' it says."

"Did he die?" Jeannette's breaths felt loud and labored as she said the words.

Yes was what the nurse had answered, and then mentioned a time in hours and minutes as if time's exactness were what mattered.

Jeannette had to pull the truck door closed twice to get it shut. "Let's get out of here." Her hair had gotten wet, and she pushed its cold dampness off her forehead. All she could think of was being home again, the warmth and soft light inside her little stone house.

Ann Marie dropped the truck into drive and they headed south through a huge swirling pool of water, then up the freeway ramp. They turned east, toward the gray clouds and beyond them the taller, darker cloud-shapes that were the Selkirk Mountains.

"You have to tell me where to turn," Ann Marie said.

"I take it you're coming with me." Jeannette thought

the drops sliding down her cheeks were from her wet hair, but when they reached her mouth, they tasted salty.

"I can always hitch home, you know. It's easier than you'd think in the rain." She shot Jeannette a glance across the seat. "Buckle that belt."

"Just take it easy, all right? Are you even old enough to drive?"

Ann Marie honked at a slow-moving mini-van in front of them, checked her side mirror, and pulled around it. "I hate to say it, but it might be better . . . in a way, I mean, if he's gone. I heard if he'd woken up, he'd be a vegetable. He wouldn't know a soul."

Jeannette sighed. "Who'd you hear that from?"

"From a friend. His mom's a nurse's aide."

Jeannette herself had heard a similar thing from Stuart's partner Mitch in the hospital hallway late one night when she'd sneaked up to Stuart's floor. She was wearing her white lab jacket, her name badge. No one questioned her. Reverend Dave had been in the room with Stuart. She'd opened the door and Dave had turned and smiled at her, his mouth still moving, finishing a sentence. Stuart's face, a huge white bundle, was turned away, toward the machines along the far wall.

Behind her in the hallway, Mitch said something about the boy being tried as an adult, while she'd stood there trying to take in everything inside Stuart's room: the pulsing monitors, Reverend Dave's low crooning prayer, the please *please* that repeated itself like the nurses' footsteps hurrying down the hall. "Please, *please*, you two, you'll have to leave now.

Only immediate family are allowed."

"So this farm where you live, are there animals?" Ann Marie asked.

"Take the next exit."

Ann Marie steered into the far right lane.

"Use the turn signal, for Pete's sake."

Ann Marie nodded and flicked it on. "Any emu?"

"Yeah, probably. Some ostrich, I think." She put her head back again. "Just go straight on this road now."

"Is there a barn up there I could maybe sleep in?"

"Barns, teepees, treehouses, whatever—you can have your pick." The girl had no idea where she was going.

Jeannette closed her eyes and let herself be rocked by the truck's bumpy, dilapidated shocks. In her mind the inside of the hospital room and the inside of the church kitchen blurred. She was stuck in that limbo between girl-friend and fiancée. What if she'd pushed open that door? Stepped into the white?

The reason she hadn't gone inside the church that January day was because she was certain, suddenly, that she'd seen the girl, the very girl here with her now. She'd been sure if she could just stare for a minute into Ann Marie's eyes, she'd know if the trouble the girl intended for Stuart was a silly prank or serious terror.

She'd seen Ann Marie and two boys standing outside the Szechwan Palace, beneath the low-hanging, red pagoda eaves. One boy had a lime green ponytail high up on his skull and below that a razed fuzz of a darker green. The other boy wore a black stocking cap. The three of them stood huddled in a little triangle, bent over something, studying it—almost certainly that voodoo doll.

Furious, Jeannette had let the church door close and hurried back down the steps. She wanted to grab that doll, snatch it out of their hands, and rip its faceless head off.

Jeannette wanted to look into the girl's eyes and tell her she was living inside an elaborate deceit. A lie of spells cast across the ice-filled Spokane River. She'd be a witch, sure, that was good, but only for a short time in this world. Because it spun so fast. Its core boiled. Juices pressed up; fissures tore open. Soon the girl would spin into her next self—if she could just get the slightest glimpse of it. She wanted to tell Ann Marie that it was time she climbed out of those dog huts. She was a young woman. She was not an animal.

In some ways she herself had been a girl like Ann Marie, lost for a while in a life she'd made up, one she could now barely connect to the person she'd become. She saw the flicker of the old Jeannette—in her waitress uniform and with a long braid down her back—as she walked toward the kids. They were brazen. It was the middle of a Friday afternoon, and Stuart's squad car was parked in the alley. They had to know he was nearby.

"Hey, shouldn't you kids be in school?" She took careful steps across the church parking lot. At its edge, between herself and them, was a four-foot-high snowbank. She peered over it.

The kids kept their heads down and huddled closer,

knitting up the edges of their little coven. The girl wore a long black wool cape with a hood.

"There ain't no school today," the girl had finally called out as if those words would stop Jeannette. "It's a teacher's conference."

"Aren't you Ann Marie, the voodoo girl?" Jeannette nodded across the snowbank as if she'd just asked her a friendly question.

"It ain't voodoo, lady. It's hoodoo."

Jeannette saw an icy bootprint in the snowbank and stuck the toe of her own brown boot into it. She stepped up, holding out her arms for balance, then stepped up again.

"Snap your fingers on her, A.M.," the boy with the ponytail said suddenly. "Snap her good and gone."

"Yeah," the other boy echoed. "Zap her." The boys laughed.

"*Don't*," Jeannette said. She'd been aiming her left foot toward the top of the snowbank, where she could see, faintly, another bootprint, but she stopped.

Ann Marie, backing away from the boys, took a step in Jeannette's direction. Beneath her fluttering cape she had on a red wool sweater. She shoved her bare hands into her cape's pockets. Her cheeks were ruddy, not like the stark white in the photograph.

"I'm a friend of Officer Duncan's." Jeannette's left foot was still dangling in the air. She realized she'd have to heave her whole body up to manage the next toehold. She took a breath, lunged.

Ann Marie watched her, steely-eyed. The boys continued staring into their hands, at what they were holding. That
doll, Jeannette thought.

"I don't do hexes anymore." Ann Marie took another
step toward Jeannette. "Those two preachers took my snake.
He had all the juju, not me."

Jeannette scanned the snowbank for the bootprints
that would lead her down the other side. But there *weren't*
any. It seemed whoever had climbed the bank before her had
simply flown off from the top into space.

She glanced down at the girl. Farther off, behind her
and the red pagoda roof, was the dog track. Battered and
barely recognizable was its old neon sign: a hunched dog,
like a swift gray shadow, halted in mid-furlong.

Jeannette herself had worked at that track—two years
ago—serving drinks in the Hound's Tooth Bar. The track
was in its heyday then, just before the mob took it over completely, before they turned the poor greyhounds' eyes a pulsing, iridescent red. The track boys said that was from "hep,"
a gooey substance injected into the dogs' long sleek necks.
Although the betting people with money—rye grass farmers
and cattle ranchers—had, after decades of droughts, a forti-
tude for risks, they believed that in the West, the odds, how-
ever harsh, should be fair: a man should be able to pass his
money through a barred window, watch it chase itself
around, and come back even greener on a good dog's head.

Wearing his crimson-and-gray Washington State
Cougars jacket, Stuart Duncan used to slip past the Hound's

Tooth's oval bar. Like a serene phantom from an urban paradise beyond hooting bettors and howling dogs, Stuart had the longest, blackest eyelashes she'd ever seen. Long before he ever kissed her, she'd wanted to feel those lashes brush her cheek. But at first he wasn't the least bit aware of her, even dressed as she was in those days in a short black skirt and black tights. She'd been someone else then: with a thick biceps—only one—in her left arm, the arm with which she hoisted her tray of drinks and kept it balanced on her palm. With her right hand, she lifted off beer mugs and shots of tequila. She might take home a hundred bucks on a good night when the hounds ran fast.

"Fuck," Ann Marie had muttered. She shook her head, staring at Jeannette stranded up there on the snow bank.

"Come on, snap her, Ann Marie," one of the boys shouted. They both busted up laughing.

Ann Marie had that defiant look Jeannette had seen so often on the faces of her neighbors at Curtain Creek. It was a look that said I'm not to be judged by your standards but only by my own. She was a girl trying to step away from bright suburbs and dark winter streets. But to where? She stood regally inside her black cape, her face as stony as a statue's.

"This Chinese place is closed, you know?" Ann Marie stabbed a foot into the snowbank, stepped up, and flung her hand toward Jeannette.

"It's been closed for years," Jeannette said. "Everything around here has." She grabbed the girl's hand and took a step down.

Ann Marie steadied her, keeping her elbow rigid. "I'll give you a tip, okay, lady?" She didn't wait for an answer. "Don't eat any red peppers or touch any silver coins for one month."

Jeannette had been concentrating so hard on digging her boot heels into the packed snow and getting to the bottom, she didn't realize that she was climbing right then out of one self and into another. She had no clue that through the coming winter she'd be cleaning the kids' teeth in the church basement and arguing with Brother Earl about giving the kids condoms, although he was happy—no problem—for her to dole out free syringes. "Do what you think is right, Jeannette," he'd said finally. "Just don't tell me about it."

"Did you hear me?" the girl had said.

"No peppers, no silver coins," Jeannette repeated and stepped down next to her. "Got it."

"*Red*. I said no *red* peppers." Ann Marie let go of her hand.

Jeannette nodded. She could see the girl's eyes, a deep hazel. As queen, the girl owned this city. The boys in army fatigues were her courtiers. Everything her royal highness was, was everything a good girl—capeless and with ordinary brown bangs—was *not*. Could not be.

"It's just a little gris-gris." Ann Marie put her hands back in her pockets. "Understand?"

"I'm *trying*," Jeannette said. She pulled off her brown suede gloves. Perhaps the girl believed that to live as someone's sweet young daughter meant to be stripped, wreathed in lilacs, and led to the fire—a sacrifice. Each May, coming into town with her neighbors to sell herbs, Jeannette had seen such girls: dressed in gowns and floated, waving, down the streets as princesses in parades. One by one, the city burned them. To have been a girl like that—not a queen, a high priestess as she was—would have been to watch the firepit being dug, the logs loaded on.

She held out the brown gloves to Ann Marie.

"The Law's going to catch the biggest fish of his whole damn life." Ann Marie tipped her head as if this were the answer to a question Jeannette had been meaning to ask. "That was my very last magic," she said. "You can tell him if you want. It's all set." She took the gloves and stuck them in her cape pocket.

Then she turned and walked back toward the boys. Her cape, as she met them, seemed to swirl them inside it. And in the span of that quick gathering-in, Jeannette saw what they'd been holding in their hands all along, what she'd assumed was the doll. One boy's hands slipped loose from it so the other boy held it by himself: a cup of espresso with its domed lid and a red straw. They'd been sharing it, warming their hands on it.

A horn blasted, and Jeannette sat up in the truck. *"What?"* she said, her heart pounding. "What?"

"Stupid dog. I hate dogs. One almost ran into the road."

"Where are we?"

"No friggin' idea."

Jeannette glanced out the window, trying to see through the rain. It was almost dark. They were passing the general store in Usk. "Just a few more miles," she told the girl. "You're doing a good job."

Ann Marie nodded. "I don't suppose there'll be any good weed up there to smoke. I don't really go for the total mind-fuck stuff, you know, just a nice mild"—she cocked her head and smiled—"buzzy buzz."

Jeannette stretched. "You'll probably find something to your liking."

"If I don't, I won't die or anything."

"Good."

The girl scrunched her face. "Oh. Sorry."

"Turn left at the Shell station." Jeannette felt exhausted, as if she'd been running all day in the rain with those wild children. But she'd spent the day scraping teeth. It was her last requirement, this practicum. She snapped thin latex gloves on and off. Slipped her hands in and out of mouths. She thought work would be good, a concentrated busyness. She'd chip loose debris around a tooth, thinking how lucky the person was not to see, up close, what she saw: the spiraling bacteria, the whirling, screw-shaped spores. Her hose sucked it all away, and as it did, she glanced into the mouth's gaping hole. "Don't worry," she'd say down the hole. "It'll soon be over. This won't hurt." Sometimes there'd be blood. She'd scour and scrape. A flap of gum would tear away.

"There'll be lambs out there," she told Ann Marie, "lots of them."

"Cool." She turned onto the gravel road, fishtailing a bit just as Jeannette herself did every time.

Jeannette filled her in a little about Curtain Creek Farm. Her mother, Kat, had been one of the founders, back in 'sixty-three, when they'd called it a commune. And her mother lived there still, just up the road from Jeannette, with Leo and his three dogs.

"God, I *hate* dogs." Ann Marie shook her head.

"That's been established." Jeannette nodded ahead. "Okay, just follow the road around. It starts to go down here."

"No shit." Ann Marie leaned forward and peered over the wheel. The road wound steeply down into the canyon, at the bottom of which the little creek ran through a meadow. In the middle of this meadow sat Jeannette's house, a small stone building that had been the pump house for a cattle ranch back in the forties.

As they went down, Ann Marie's eyes widened. "This is wild," she said. "It's like a big crack in the ground."

At the bottom the air was thick with woodsmoke, and the canyon road slick, muddy. The potholes had filled with rain and the truck's tires went *whomp, whomp* as they slogged through. "I guess you better stay at my place for now," Jeannette said. "I can make us some sandwiches."

"Not *tuna*. Please." Ann Marie wrinkled her nose.

Jeannette turned and studied the girl's face. She had a softly curved head, a subtle jut of chin. In the dusky light, with the snake shape less discernible, her skull seemed hued with deep purples and greens.

They passed Roxanne's school-bus house, where Big

Dog, unfazed by the rain, lay sleeping on the roof. He raised his head and barked once as the truck went by.

"Was that a dog or a wolf?"

Jeannettte shrugged. "Hard to say."

They passed Rollie in his tattered straw hat. He was wrapping a plastic tarp around his cornstalk teepee. The teepee was his new experiment. He'd dug a shit hole inside it.

"Man, you weren't kidding about the treehouse. Do people live up there?" Ann Marie slowed and stared out the window at the two huge maples that supported five or six rooms, all connected by plank bridges.

"You better go faster through here or we'll get stuck."

Jeannette pointed and they pulled into the drive outside her house. Behind it, the meadow was slicked down by the rain. "Leave your shoes on the stoop," Jeannette said as she kicked off her own and went in. She lit the kerosene lamp and laid some kindling in the woodstove. She took the dental tools from her pocket and set them in a china bowl.

Ann Marie went to the sink and stood staring at it, a glass in her hand.

"You have to pump that handle a few times," Jeannette told her. Soon the water flowed.

Ann Marie made the sandwiches. Cheese and butter on bread. Jeannette studied hers for a minute, thinking she couldn't possibly eat, but after she'd taken a bite, she found it was exactly what she wanted. The butter was thick on the bread, sweet and rich.

"Did you think it was my fault, I mean at first, when it happened?" Ann Marie set her plate in the sink.

"It might have crossed my mind. But then they caught that boy right away." Jeannette was still chewing slowly, standing on the wood floor, which felt damp and cold through her socks.

Ann Marie pumped more water and watched it fill her glass.

"Here at the Farm some of the oldtimers call themselves anarchists, but that's sort of a joke now. No one breaks any rules here. Not any big ones." Jeannette set her plate on top of Ann Marie's in the sink. She wanted to explain something, but wasn't sure what. "The city," she said, "it's all chaos now. People think it isn't, but it is."

Outside, the rain fell in torrents. She hung up a hammock for Ann Marie, who, even as she lay back in it, was full of questions. How had Jeannette met Stuart? Where did they go on dates? She wanted a story, a story about romance, about love.

"'I hear you're going to testify,' were the first words he said to me," Jeannette told her. "I was wiping tables at the Hound's Tooth Bar. It was the last night there. A couple guys were already on ladders, boarding up windows. 'You're a brave girl.' That's what Stuart said next. I'd been subpoenaed. It was rumored, though, that the track owners were already in Brazil. But I was still scared of them. There wasn't much they wouldn't do for money. I told Stuart they gave the dogs drugs. I'd whispered that like it was some big secret. 'Really?' he said. I was so stupid. I never dreamed he was a cop."

"He wasn't wearing his uniform, huh?"

Telling the story seemed to revive Jeannette. She mentioned the leather Cougars jacket. That night Stuart had sat at a table with Red, one of the track regulars. Slumped in their chairs, they'd kept their eyes on the dogs, watching out the last unboarded window. The dogs were still huffing and puffing as the track boys gave them their final post-parade blanket and muzzle inspections.

At the next table the track owners had been slipping rubber bands off six-inch wads of twenties, getting the presidents' faces all staring up in the same direction. From Red's table, Stuart turned and smiled across at the towers of money. What in the world would have made her guess he was a cop?

That night he'd watched her swab tables. Outside, the dogs whined. She'd taken her time. It had felt good to have him see her. As she worked, her braid swung across her back like a pendulum ticking itself down to stillness.

As she told Ann Marie the story, she saw again those stacks of twenties. The taller those towers, the faster the dogs ran. The fired gun flipped the switch, and the dogs' noses aimed the dogs' bodies round and round. The plastic bunny bobbed on a wire, always just a bite away. Stretching toward it, the dogs' powerful haunches set the sky in motion. Inside the track's oval stood the assorted flags of a world no one cared about. The great dog-machine, cranking into operation, whipped up its own wind and made the flags flap.

Over the bar that last night she'd seen on the TV late news that forty-six dogs were about to be left—*homeless*, the newsman said. Many were sick, malnourished. She'd been transitioning then too, slipping from one Jeannette to another. A *transmigration*, she thought now—an untouched part of her roused, attaching itself at that moment to someone the previous Jeannette wouldn't have believed she could love. On TV the dogs seemed pale without their brightly colored racing jackets. She imagined them running, late, through downtown Spokane, nipping at the ankles of symphony-goers, yapping in the alleys behind the banks where the smell of money would be as familiar to them as dog chow.

"Let me walk you to your car," Stuart said when she'd turned off the lights over the bar.

He'd helped her carry boxes of canned vegetables, items the cook gave away to anyone who'd worked that last shift. She'd still believed then that he was an ordinary guy. As they walked across the employee parking lot, she kicked aside a syringe. Stuart watched it skitter over the asphalt, its orange-tipped plunger shining. He blinked, flashing his eyelashes, while all around, the dogs—sick, winded, lonely—howled in their little huts.

A week later she'd seen him again. In the courtroom. Sitting in his dress blues. The bright silver badge. She felt as if someone had hung her upside down and sucked the air out. She'd answered a dozen questions from the D.A., asked in a voice that was way too loud. Stuart had nodded to her.

She looked up. Ann Marie's hammock was perfectly

still, and Jeannette couldn't tell if she'd fallen asleep or was still listening to the story.

Jeannette opened the stove door and dropped two logs inside, then banked the coals so the fire would burn through the night. She put on a flannel nightgown. Outside, the rain continued pouring. The last thing she thought about as she lay down was Stuart's ulcer. It was like a hole in a tooth no one could patch. It could bleed. A teenage boy's head lice could make it bleed. A girl's bruised cheek.

The next sound she heard was in her dream, a slosh-slosh. A nice sound. Gentle. It was the sound of drinks on a tray carried high over her head. "Want to split a quinella with me?" an old woman at the bar asked. She was dragging an oxygen tank behind her, its tubes in her nose. "No thanks," Jeannette answered, "I'm saving my dimes. I have six classes to finish at the Dental Academy." She quizzed herself as she worked, going over vocabulary—not for teeth, but for religion class. Molars she knew, bicuspids, and how to measure the thickness of gums. But for religion class, she carried flashcards. *Transmigration, Transubstantiation, Transmogrification.* What is it when the soul flees the body? What's the body eating the soul? The body becoming another body? She had the answers in her black skirt pocket. She'd nod to the man in the Cougars jacket, but he wasn't seeing her. Not yet.

In her dream she rocked. Snow fell, and through the wet white flakes a black hand swooped down. With its wide palm and long elegant fingers, it touched Stuart's shoulder, once, twice. It was the sort of hand someone coming in from an alley and glimpsing through an open doorway might have believed to be a hand of God.

Slosh-slosh went the dream. Her bed rocked. It seemed lifted off the stone floor. She sat up, and the bed rocked harder. And then she saw: the foot-high bed legs were *not* on the floor.

She stepped down and splashed into the cold. "Whoa!" she shouted and was suddenly fully awake.

"What?" Ann Marie called from the hammock. "*What?*"

"It's the creek. It's come in." Wet and rank, the water pressed her nightgown to her calves. Her white lab jacket, its sleeves billowing, floated by like a drowned person with his head and legs below water.

She lit the lamp and sat back down on the wobbling bed, then turned and glanced out the window behind her. The moon flashed from behind a cloud, a frail sickle, then disappeared again into the dark.

Ann Marie sat up in the hammock.

"Don't," Jeannette said. "Don't get down in this muck. Let's just think a minute. Let's not do anything right now."

"Fine by me. Hey look, all your teeth tools. In that bowl."

Lying on her belly on the mattress, Jeannette leaned into the water and caught the bowl of them as it bobbed by. She set the bowl on a high bookshelf. Then she got on her knees on the bed and opened the window. She couldn't see anything out there. Blackness over blackness. If the water got any higher inside, they'd have to go out there. Out the window.

Then they heard the bell. Jeannette had heard it twice before—both times for fires, a grass fire once and then a house fire. "Okay," she said. "That's it. Let's go."

Without hesitating, Ann Marie climbed down from the hammock. "Yick," she said when she stepped into the water.

Jeannette arched one leg out the window, then the other, and lowered herself into the black icy water. It came up to her waist.

Ann Marie leapt from the window, laughing as she hit the water. She clutched Jeannette's nightgown. "Fuck," she sang, laughing again.

Sonny, Jeannette's neighbor, was suddenly close by in a skiff. She helped them into it. They had to crawl over a bale of hay in the middle of the boat. "I'll get you girls to Kat's house in two minutes," Sonny said, passing them a dry blanket. They sat shivering, huddled together, the blanket around their shoulders as Sonny revved the motor and headed the boat into what had been the pasture.

"Who's that crying?" Ann Marie asked. The sound was coming from straight ahead.

Jeannette was shivering too hard to speak. That's where we're going, she wanted to say, out there to the sheep, which must have climbed up, somehow, on the rocks of the canyon wall.

Then the moon slipped back out, and as the boat churned through the water, they could see people, people swimming in the water—Rollie, Scooter, Don, and then Leo.

"What the hell are they *doing?*" Ann Marie said.

Now they could make out the sheep in the water, too. Sheep with people's arms around their necks and bellies. Her neighbors were swimming the sheep across to higher ground.

"The water's way past my fences," Sonny shouted over the whir of the motor. She pushed her thick glasses up her nose and pointed to the bale and then to the rocky cliffs. "Just a quick delivery. This hay'll shut them up."

Her teeth chattering loudly, Jeannette now caught sight of the sheep perched on the canyon cliffs. Suddenly unfenced and unhoused, the sheep, which stood leaning and baahing on the sharp basalt ledges, looked ready to topple over at any moment.

Sonny spread the hay on the rocks, and the sheep stepped down and nosed into it, crying and eating at the same time, although now their cries were softer.

A half hour later, Jeannette and Ann Marie were warming themselves by the roaring fire in Kat's stone fireplace. Kat gave them dry clothes. All through the pre-dawn hours, neighbors drifted in, bringing blankets and beer. By the time the roosters started crowing, Leo's three dogs had run themselves silly out front, barking their heads off, as neighbors— in canoes, kayaks, rowboats— paddled back and forth across the meadow.

"Kind of a nice lake," Ann Marie said later that morning when they were out on the water again, this time in Leo's rubber raft.

And it was true. Her mother's house, up the hillside, now resembled a nice little resort on a nice little lake. They were returning from taking dry clothes and blankets to neighbors who'd set up a huge tent on the opposite shore from the sheep. There was a sweet smell of woodsmoke through the canyon. The sun shone fiercely. A mother osprey flew over, circled the new lake, taunting the sheep, her shrill cries flung down at their low baahs. The bird loved it, loved it all.

Jeannette pulled the oars. Just ahead of them, in a truck tire's inner-tube, two boys were using Ping-Pong paddles to row themselves toward a blue propane tank that lurked like a half-submerged submarine in the water.

Ann Marie waved to the boys. Her purple-and-green skull shimmered. She wanted to try rowing. But her oar strokes just made parentheses in the water.

Jeannette smiled at her. "Try pulling straight back. Slow and straight."

Putting her shoulders into it, Ann Marie managed to move them forward a few feet, then a few more.

Jeannette nodded and sat back, surveying the lake. The frozen meadow of the canyon had simply filled with water like a deep bowl. Somewhere beneath the new lake, she knew, was the old creek—a black vein, a current. Maybe they'd crossed it and maybe they hadn't.

And surely she'd brought on this rain: grieving for Stuart last night in her dreams. The water of *her*. Calling out to more water. She'd helped make this lake, a lake of tears, but soon, soon, if they were lucky, it would all drain back into the warmed-up earth.

"My mother wants us to take Leo's truck and make a

supply run into Cusick." Jeannette reached forward and took the oars from Ann Marie.

Ann Marie sighed and tipped her face back into the sunlight. "Think we can get an espresso there?"

"Sure." In her own voice she heard a familiar tone, one she used when she spoke to a child in the dental chair: *It's almost over now, honey. Take it easy. You're just about done.*

The supplies were for the flood party that would take place later that night. That's what you did at the Farm after a catastrophe; you had a party. Her mother had made a list: brownies, ice cream, chips, beer.

But at the party that night, there was a very different sort of spread: homemade pies and cookies and a few bottles of home-brewed raspberry wine. Jeannette and Ann Marie stood on the porch and watched the slim moon float up over the lake. Inside, the party was in full swing. They could hear Kat saying, "Okay, on the count of three, I'm going to snap my fingers, and you'll wake up. One, two, three." She was bringing someone out of a hypnotic trance.

"Are you going to do that?" Ann Marie asked Jeannette. "Let her put you under?"

"Nah, I've done it a million times. Are you?"

"No. I'm way past that now." She lit a stub of a cigarette she'd evidently smoked halfway down sometime earlier. "No more. Finito." She inhaled.

"Yeah," Jeannette said, "I'm finally getting it."

"So do you think I could stay here for a few more days?

Just, you know, to chill." Ann Marie's eyes were bright hazel dots in the dim light.

"In all this mess?" Jeannette swept her arm in the direction of the water.

Ann Marie exhaled a long silvery puff. "As bad as it is out here right now, it seems pretty good to me."

Jeannette nodded at the water. "Okay," she said. She turned to Ann Marie. "It'll be fine, I guess. It'll be all right."

From inside the house came peals of laughter. Her neighbor Roxanne was Rolfing Leo's neck. Alison had stuck sweet-smelling lilies of the valley in everyone's hair. And now Scooter was speaking in a Scottish accent, reciting a poem he claimed he'd written back when he was Robert Burns in 1788:

> Till all the seas gone dry, my dear,
>   And the rocks melt with the sun!
> And I will love Thee still, my dear,
>   While the sands o' life shall run.
>
> And fare Thee well, my only love,
>   And fare Thee well awhile!
> And I will come again, my love,
>   Though it were ten thousand mile!

Ann Marie looked at Jeannette and rolled her eyes. She stubbed out her cigarette.

Inside, the neighbors were laughing, but out there on

the porch, Jeannette was crying. She hadn't yet told her mother about Stuart's death. She hadn't told anyone. Kat had enough to cope with just then. They all had.

Ann Marie went to her and draped an arm around her shoulders. Jeannette let herself lean into the girl.

"He was a good guy," Ann Marie said. "I never meant for him to be gone, not gone . . . like this." She patted Jeannette's arm. "No way like this."

Jeannette tipped her head back, and they both watched a cloud slip across the scythe of the moon. The spot of warmth on her shoulder from Ann Marie's hand was the only warm place on her body.

The flood of Curtain Creek had been bad, but in Cusick that afternoon, she and Ann Marie had seen the real thing. The Pend Oreille River had jumped its banks and poured over the highway's black asphalt. Standing by Leo's pickup, they'd watched the rushing rapids carry off a dead tabby cat, a toilet, a cow, and several trees that had been lifted, roots and all, from the earth.

The Cusick store had been empty, a wall of sandbags blocking the door. Half a block away, people were piling bags in front of the Township School's double doors. Jeannette recognized a few neighbors from the Farm. They were wearing the thick gray felted coats made from Sonny's sheep's wool.

"Oh good, here you are at last," someone had said to her. She turned and saw Rollie. He seemed to have been expecting her. He gave a quick tug to Ann Marie's jacket. "Step on in here now, girls."

Behind them more people had quickly gathered, and suddenly she and Ann Marie were drawn into the action, links in a chain of hands.

"Heave ho," Rollie called and tossed Jeannette a sandbag. It pulled her hands down hard when she caught it so that she almost toppled forward. Rollie smiled and tugged on his straw hat. "I'm guessing the worst is about over."

Jeannette kept looking back at the river. It was trying to make itself into something bigger, mightier, crazier than it had been.

"Someone mentioned there's a party later," Rollie said. "At your mother's place. Is that right?" He bent his knees and stooped toward another bag.

She studied his rhythm. She had to get herself in synch with these baggers. It was all in the timing—the catching and the letting go.

"Yep," she said, and leaned into Rollie's toss, catching the bag neatly. "We're supposed to be getting supplies." She let the bag's weight yank her low; then she lifted herself and the bag up together, in one big sweep.

"Well, the hell with that," Rollie said, and his laugh echoed back at the loud rush of water. "We've got as much back there as we need."

The breath Jeannette took seemed to help her hoist up the weight at her feet. And "Heave ho," she called as the bag went flying from her hands into the next pair, Ann Marie's, which rose to meet it.

THE LAP OF LUXURY

(Geneva)

Russell was telling the three of us—Melody, Leigh, and me—a story, a true story, and the three of us were crying, but Russell wasn't. It was an account of the last moments of his mother's life. His face was pale, not its usual ruddy hue as if he'd just come in from jogging. His brown eyes seemed more deeply set in his face. Perhaps that was the grief, I thought, or maybe it was the way he was aging now, out of boyhood, into his late twenties.

I couldn't look away from him. I didn't care about the single tear tediously dredging a path down my cheek. I was struck by Russell's composure, his concentration on telling the tale in the face of three women's sorrow. We sat in his mother's two-room house. We dabbed at our eyes—all three together. A choreography from a Greek tragedy.

Russell pressed his palms against his knees. "'*I'm still here, aren't I?*' That's what she said." He looked up from his hands, and at me. "'*I'm still right here.*' The nurse had drawn the curtain around us. I felt we were inside a cavern. I'd come

out again, but she wouldn't. And that's just what happened."
He shook his head.

"And what did *you* say, honey?" Melody asked him.

"I just answered her. I said, '*Yes, Mom. You're here.*' But I don't think she heard me."

"She didn't know if she was here or gone." Leigh folded her lace hanky, its corners embroidered with blue flowers.

Melody and I had spongy tissues balled up in our fists. Russell's mother, Lila, had been our friend and neighbor for most of our adult lives. If we added up all the hours, we'd probably spent a good year standing ankle-deep in Curtain Creek with Lila, washing onions, leeks, potatoes.

"She heard you, Russ." I stood up, walked across the room, and threw my tissue into Lila's woodstove. For a year, when Russell was a baby, I'd slept near that stove, on a mat on the floor. If Lila was too tired to get up to change him, I would. I fed him homemade baby food from our harvests: mashed carrots, green beans, applesauce.

When I turned back, Leigh and Melody were each putting a hand in their jeans pockets, and Russell's eyes snapped from them to me, imploring. His mouth opened.

"None of that now, girls," I said. "Russ is all grown up now."

Years ago, when he was about to return to college after a visit home, Melody and Leigh would empty the change from their pockets into his hands. But this time Melody only produced a fresh tissue and Leigh held up a roll of breath mints. The false alarm made the three of us smile at him through our tears.

Russell rolled his eyes. He'd be on his way in a few days, not back to his laboratory job across the state in Seattle, but out into the swamps of Minnesota, where high school kids had come upon a dozen translucent frogs. The Northern Leopard Frog had disappeared from ninety-five percent of its habitat, Russell told me yesterday, but ozone depletion was probably not the main cause. "It's not just solar radiation zapping those frog eggs, Geneva," he said. "Other factors are at work. Trust me. Nothing's that simple." And although he was a biologist now, a herpetologist, to be exact, in his threadbare jeans and patched flannel shirt, he still looked like any one of us from Curtain Creek.

Lila had been under the earth for two days—two days of chilling November rains, biting, stinging rains. Just getting to a consensus about her burial had been a major feat. No one that young—only fifty—was supposed to be dead. None of us at the Farm had been prepared. For thirty years she'd lived among us, struggled with us to safeguard all we believed in and worked for. This valley of our personal freedom lay carved out between two snowcapped ridges. Our hands were calloused, our nails ragged, dirty. Sometimes we'd go for days without saying a word to another human being, lost in a quiet dailiness: shelling peas, peeling pearl onions.

Lila's death didn't just sadden us; it frightened us. The white uniforms, the whiter shoes, chemo, ticking monitors, inscrutable pain—from nowhere they suddenly loomed before us. Even together, we were lonely. All the organic beans and tomatoes, all the tofu curries and the raw rolled barley in the world would not save us if they had not saved her—our Lila, studious observer of leaf mold and bug rot.

By October, we knew she didn't have much longer. The cancer was sending out tendrils, choking off her liver and kidneys. "This question of what to do with Lila's body is bringing out the worst in us," I had said at a monthly residents' meeting. Only occasionally did I attend these meetings. I hadn't been living on the Farm for a dozen years, but I still kept my cabin there, and sometimes on weekends I drove out from town. "We're a community here," I said. "We need a cemetery. Kids need a place to mourn their loved ones."

"That's not who we are, Geneva. That's a whole Christian trip," Reuben said, "the sacred remains and all that." Then he reminded us that a cemetery would be nothing more than a throwback to the society we'd abandoned. Adulation of the afterlife. When it was this life—yes, we all believed it was this life—that counted.

"But we just can't go around burning bodies either. That sucks," Roxanne said. "Even cave people buried their dead."

The arguments swirled over our heads. At last Rollie, who was nearing seventy, stood up and took off his straw hat. The top of his bald head was starkly white above his tanned face. "We've looked out for one another, many of us here, since nineteen sixty-seven. Shared food, firewood." He turned the hat in his hands. Three bird feathers—bright orange, iridescent blue, chalk white—stuck up from the hatband. "Please. Cemetery or no cemetery, we have to stand together in death, too. You can put Lila in my back field. Hell, I don't mind. I've always loved her."

*   *   *

Russell had reached his right hand toward my left ear. Could this have been only six months ago? He'd touched my earring, a tiny amethyst dangling at the bottom of a silver hoop. "Those suckers could catch one primo brown trout." His fingers were cool against my neck.

I took a quick breath.

"Does it bother you when I touch you?" He was home for a summer visit, and from our booth in the Red Rail Tavern, we were watching Lila and her new boyfriend Wayne dancing on the dusty floor.

"Not *bother*. Not exactly." I shook my head.

He poked my earring gently so it jingled. "No?"

Then I smiled, which I shouldn't have done. Every tiny gesture from me toward him seemed to occur too quickly, like slippages, leakages. "It's dangerous."

Russell leaned toward me, serious, his eyes such a dark shade of brown they almost matched his black hair. "Tell me to stop then."

We'd had this conversation before. On and off, five years running.

"Gen." He leaned closer. "Tell me to stop."

"You two. *Honestly*." Lila had returned to our table. She laughed. Wayne stood behind her, his hand on her back.

The hunched buffalo on his belt buckle caught the light from a flickering bar sign.

Russell let his hand fall slowly from my earring to the table.

"I bet you heard my head crack against that post just now, huh?" Lila asked us.

"I doubt it," Wayne said. "They seem otherwise engaged."

I shook my head.

"You *didn't?* You didn't see Wayne spin me right out into that wooden post? *Conk!* Lordy, I was seeing stars. I thought everyone in here must have heard. It's just lucky I'm not passed out."

"Maybe you are, Mom. Maybe you are and you just don't know it." Russell slid a finger around the rim of his beer mug.

Lila was six years older than I was, and Russell was fifteen years younger. Just a week before that night at the Red Rail, Lila had told me as we sat on her porch stoop that, as far as she was concerned, this age business didn't mean crap. "Hell, Wayne is nine years younger than me. Frank was eight years older. It's all a bunch of hooey." She'd put her hand on my arm. Neither of us had even a hint then that we'd soon be sitting in the same spot deciding at what point Russell and I should tell her doctors to take the machines away. "The years keep mushing us closer, Gen," she said that night. "It gets blurrier and blurrier. Russ is stubborn as all get-out. He just won't get over you."

"He'll find someone. Someone who likes frogs."

Lila patted my arm. "We don't know that. We don't." She whistled once and her dog came and stood in front of us. We scratched his ears. "Russell's been out into the world, Geneva. Like you have. But he comes home, doesn't he?"

In the tavern the next week I kept remembering how I'd nodded *yes*. What was the question? Lila and Wayne did the twist, squirming lower and lower. Even with the kind of liberty I'd lived my life for, weren't there limits? Could a middle-aged woman really put her head back against the red vinyl booth and let the electricity go haywire when a young man's fingers slipped across her chin, down her neck?

"There are these big scales with huge weights piling up on both sides," I told Russ, "and I don't know which side to hop on to tilt it one way or another."

"Then let me," he said. "I know."

I pointed to a young girl at the bar. "Okay, now what about her? That cute redhead? Go up there and order something. Talk to her."

"Not interested." He picked up my hand. He pressed my fingers. "Give me some credit, Geneva."

I'd been right there at his birth. I'd never told him, and I doubted Lila recalled it, but I'd been the one to give him the last gentle tug that pulled him out of her and into the world. Rain on her tin roof, and me with both hands around his neck, trying to pull him and not choke him at the same time. I had no idea what I was doing. I'd helped Sonny pull a lamb out once, but that was it. I was almost sixteen and had been on the Farm only for a month. Two guys, Scooter and Don, had found me in Pike Street Market in Seattle, where they were selling organic vegetables. With their similar sets of bad black teeth, they looked strangely related. They still do. Back at the Farm it was the potato harvest, they'd told me, and I could help out. They were expecting a bumper crop, and they could use every digger they could get. "We work sunup to sundown," they'd warned me. When the harvest was over, I'd have to leave. They didn't have any spare houses or extra rooms. "Girl," they called me the whole way back across the state. "Let the girl sleep in the back. She looks whacked out."

Just before the baby came, Lila had been smoking a cigar-sized reefer with Scooter and Don. To ease the pain, they'd told her, as they put it in her mouth. Don had cut the baby's cord with the same kitchen knife I'd used an hour earlier to slice up an apple.

*   *   *

But I did stay at the Farm—for twelve years. My cabin, six by eight feet, had a window in the roof—a window that filled with moonlight at two a.m. My single bed was suspended by ropes from the ceiling. When, at seventeen, I'd moved out of Lila's to live there, I used to stand by the doorway at dawn, listening to the rooster and watching a silver-winged osprey glide over the potato fields, headed due east to the Pend Oreille River. I drank my strong coffee. In another hour I'd be unearthing Yukon Golds by Curtain Creek.

"Holy smokes, it's like finding treasure," I told Rollie when he'd first showed me how to dig with the potato fork. He still had a few wisps of salt-and-pepper hair then, long and slicked back under his straw hat. I dug the fork in slowly, carefully, under the weight of my heel. The earth sucked it down. I loved that feel. Then I'd pull back on the fork and open the dirt-vault. I'd kneel and rake my fingers toward the edges, past the big cold oval potatoes, for what we all loved best: the tiny potato eggs, the babies, nudged to the far perimeters, tethered by thin runners. Those small ones we'd later wrap in foil and set on the coals of our harvest fires. Then we'd top them with goat cheese or rich, buttery browned onions. Sometimes there'd be a special tea, brewed with mushrooms Scooter and Don had brought back from the coast, from the rain forest there, and we'd sip and watch each other's pupils grow as big as quarters. Howling and hooting. The Farm's children were barefoot, their cornhusk dolls lined up by castles of bark and rock.

And everywhere the dogs. For years they'd been the coyotes' lovers in the hills, so the pups that licked our feet were half wild. But they came if we called sweetly, and they sat with us for a while by the fire. They let us scratch their ears. When it was late, the moon dangling low and the children wrapped in blankets, asleep among the spent day lilies, we'd begin a shedding of clothes. Lila was always first to unveil. Her nipples were bright pink beads circling the fire. We were no longer in our right minds, and glad of it. The triangles of pubic hair—brown, black, yellow—were secret runes beside the red embers. The moonlight made us glisten.

Big Dog had selected Lila. Lila was sure his father was a wolf and his mother one of Leo's black Labs; I told her the father was probably just a no-account coyote. Big Dog ate scraps, even beet greens. He gnawed on corn cobs. On winter nights he came down from the snowy ridgetops and slept on Lila's porch. The gray spots on his black-and-tan coat had lightened. Up there, prowling in the snow, no doubt he blended in with the wintry trees.

Two days ago when Lila was safely settled in the ground, fifty yards from the beehives she loved and from which she was the only one brave enough to gather honey, and after her marker of blue telephone insulators had been fused together atop her grave, Big Dog became everyone's. Melody said she couldn't look at him without thinking of Lila. Some nights he slept at Melody and Leigh's and sometimes down past the lower thirty at Leo and Kat's. Or he slept outside my cabin, his back pressed up close to the wall nearest my small kerosene heater. I stayed there too—while Russell stayed up the dirt road at his mother's place. I imagined him pacing as he did when he was pondering a problem about the frogs, pacing around Lila's cactus plants, pausing now and then to sort through her papers. My heater hissed. Big Dog's snores outside were like the snores of a very old man.

*   *   *

Lila was the one who'd made me go back to high school. I'd lost my whole sophomore year traveling—hitching rides, going wherever someone else, some stranger, was going. At the Farm, Lila, with Rollie's expert assistance, arranged everything, improvising documents with a new name for me. "Father unknown," one paper said.

"Good," I told her. "Good deal." I rode the school bus with the happy teenagers, watching them whisper and giggle, and feeling more like an old aunt than one of them. Back then, the Farm had a tutor for the younger children, and they sang songs in French down by the creek, caught bugs, and drew maps of the world in the mud. In a few years Russell would be one of those kids—barefoot, running after a dog that was chasing a rabbit through the pungent leeks.

Even then my own childhood had seemed years and miles away, tangled in red mangrove roots, half-submerged in the salty marsh waters in the Florida Keys. Sometimes in the dim early light as I rode the bus over rain-dampened roads that twisted and rose up out of our valley, I could almost smell again the girl I'd been, my hair wet and full of sand. The girl who'd stood alone under a light bulb and smashed a chair across a kitchen table, watched the legs fly off and the seat and back drop in pieces at her feet. I could see my stepfather's short red hair, shorter still beneath the white Coast Guard cap, before the cap sailed across the room. I was a child pressed into his service. His grip on my shoulder and hip made matching blue tattoos. I belonged to him like a canal dredged out deep for the big white pleasure boats, their black flags flapping in the oceanic wind.

Before she put me on the yellow bus, Lila had sent me to see Melody and Leigh, who lived just past the ice hut in a domed house. Melody and Leigh had pulled out two boxes—low and flat—from under their bed. Inside were dozens of shoes, the pairs held together by rubber bands. Melody passed Leigh various pairs of shoes, and Leigh would put them on my feet: red pumps, black loafers, soft brown oxfords with laces. The dome house was sweltering. With such interminable sunlight, it almost always was. The shoes, I knew, were still there—many of them the same sturdy pairs kids had worn a decade ago and others would wear again. I'd put on the brown ones and smiled. Melody and Leigh motioned me to walk around, and my footsteps circled a braided rug's circumference. That day, while still a teenager, I'd begun to sense some small perpetuity—those shoes slipped on and kicked off, going round and round.

After two years at the high school, I managed to make my way, slowly, through the community college, then the state university, where they gave me a work-study program and left me alone in the art studio. My job was to keep it tidy. That's where I'd learned to make paper—cooking it, steaming shredded willow branches. Grasses whirled in a blender with paprika and celery seeds. Bark paper. As Lila said about me then, I was all over the map.

Even now I've been known to get eight blenders going at once in my studio, which is also my living space, atop the old newsprint storage building in downtown Spokane. The owner couldn't believe I wanted to live up here. Still, he helped me rig up a toilet and sink to the ancient plumbing, shaking his head the whole time. I could grab a shower at the Y after a swim, no problem, I told him. To me, after twelve years at the Farm, it seemed the very lap of luxury.

With my blenders plugged into a power strip, I was set. The paper I made became my lampshades—tall triangular ones and cylindricals wrapped around a strutted framework of red dogwood saplings. I embellished the shades with pine needles, varnished leaves onto them. These became hot items in Seattle and Sante Fe. I boxed them up. I shipped them out.

Weekends, out on the Farm, suspended in my bed under the moonlight, I thought of new wrinkles: wheat cherubs, one leg in and one out of a lampshade. Big Dog snored. If I stepped outside, he came for me to scratch his ears, which I did, but he soon turned away. My hands weren't hers. I wasn't Lila.

The gallery owner in Sante Fe has told me he can't imagine why I don't just pack up my blenders and move on down there, where the endless sunshine on the ocher mountains should surely provide a steady source of my kind of light. It's a nice light, all right, I've told him on the phone. I've been there. I've seen it. But too much of a good thing isn't good anymore. I couldn't explain this to a man whose eyes are glued all day to a cash register. When I visited there, the high-heeled clerks in the boutiques wouldn't look at me in my black overalls and red sneakers, although I had, oddly enough, the same-sized wad of cash in my pockets as browsing women in their sequined silk cowgirl shirts.

Spokane was a city of no pretenses. No one, thank God, had tried to save its downtown yet. Its ugly heart still beat wildly, and bankers still snubbed the hobos just off the freight trains from Portland or Great Falls. Green-haired, safety-pin-lipped teenagers skateboarded down the center of First Avenue, where old lady shoppers, crossing the street, gave them a wide berth. Buses chugged and burped a foul smoke, and no one cared. It was, as Russell often said, "a what*ever* kind of place."

In a few days he'd be off to Minnesota where kids had found the see-through frogs. Also several club-footed frogs. A frog with nine little legs. Russell kept getting phone calls.

"More trouble in the lily pads," he'd say when he hung up.

He showed me a photograph from his backpack. "See, this frog has an eye in its throat."

I squinted down. "Its *own* eye?"

"See that bulge in its neck? And its two regular eyes are sealed shut."

I stared at the puffy throat that would never croak, at the bugged-out eyes that didn't have a clue about sky, water, pond muck. "He's so *white*."

"Their skin's water-permeable, and this particular kind overwinters, so he stays submerged for a long time. Down deep. His immune system's shot."

Russell put the photograph back in his pack. "There're eleven more just like him up there." His theory, when he explained it to me, had to do with heavy metals concentrated on the bottoms of those marshes, pollutants from herbicides and fertilizers the local sorghum farmers used. "It all drifts down." He shook his head. "It drifts down and drifts down."

What he saw in his everyday life was ugly, I thought, sad and ugly. I touched his arm.

He turned to me, lifted my fingers to his mouth and kissed them, one by one.

*   *   *

At the farmer's market in Spokane I used to push my table up close to Lila's—mine with its lamps and hers with its vegetables. This way we could talk when the shoppers thinned out. On her table were plastic Baggies of pea pods, red basil, catnip, peppermint. There were tidy rows of turnips, beets, potatoes. *Organically Loved*, the sign behind her read. The farmer's market was how I got my start. One day a gallery owner from Seattle, a man with a gold-tipped cane, had stopped and bought a few of my lamps to take home, to "test the waters," he said.

When things were slow, Lila would tell me about Russell, whom I rarely saw then. I was in college. I'd already burned out the motors in three blenders, and number four wasn't long for the world. From Curtain Creek's runoff, Russell had collected all manner of salamanders, tadpoles, and water bugs. He knew how they breathed and ate and procreated. "Surely he doesn't get that sort of smartness from me," Lila said.

"Then who?" I'd asked. Maybe after so many years, the secrecy about Russell's father's identity wasn't still an issue. But she'd only stared at me, then shrugged as she always had. She ran her hands across the beets.

Now I had gold-embossed cards that said *Geneva Lamps*, as though they weren't created by a person but by a place.

Which was true in a way. The place of the lamps was a stand of red dogwood that grows along Curtain Creek; it was those quaking aspens, their silver saplings tied and soaking by my ankles in the creek's icy water; and it was the circle of grass on which Russell had stood when he set down his bucket of toads, the summer after he'd finished college, and said my name in a new way. There, for a few moments, I was the woman he saw before him. I stepped out of the chill to approach him, and everything radiated out from my cold toes in the damp grass.

He bent and cupped first my left foot, then my right, in his warm hands. "It's too soon to be wading around in that creek, Geneva. What were you thinking?" Then he blew three warm breaths on my toes the way someone might blow on icy fingers.

"I guess there's still snow on Cee Cee Ah Mountain, isn't there?" We looked up at its white bowler.

And my lamps were from up there too, from the high plateaus' blue-green shoots and grasses, from the cold swirls of snow, the warm grass-breaths. In all these places the light settled, and I gathered it in.

So many diggers. We took turns with the shovels. I couldn't help remembering emptying the treasure vaults and the mounds of potatoes in wooden crates I'd help pile on carts. Rollie had made the casket himself. It sat like a burned-out sun pulling us toward it, our emptied-out Lila inside. As we dug, the rain hammered down between the ridges, deepening our valley, our world that had become incomparably present as the weight of what was gone from us dropped out of it. Farewell.

Or wasn't she still here? Still right here. In our fogged breaths. In the rain on our slickers streaked with dirt, sweet pungent dirt, clattering against the pine box.

We were all submerged under that weight when it went down. Rollie had used ten shiny belt-buckles for simple embellishments over the lid's nails. One was a buffalo buckle, given by Wayne, who had loved her last. He stood with Russell across the cavernous hole from me.

The dozen young children from the Farm, who'd never seen a burial before, stared at the adults as we dabbed our eyes. Melody and Leigh on either side of me took my hands.

Good-bye. The *good* is what was, what's passed. Behind us. And the *bye* moves us along, onward, past the past. It's a whispered word, a raised hand. I watched Russell across the abyss of the grave. His eyes were rain-darkened, cast down. Down and down. Toward Lila. Still her. Still here. She loved that ground.

*　　*　　*

Russell takes the service elevator up to the top floor of my building. I hear the pulleys creak and groan. The elevator, which used to haul up bales of newsprint, makes the whole floor I stand on shimmy. I wait for Russell's knock. In the last hour the rain has turned to sleet, then to snow, back to sleet, and now rain again.

Russell says he wants to say good-bye to me before he flies off to the frogs in Minnesota. I know that, coming in my alleyway door, he's had to step over Ed, the wino who sleeps there. It was Ed's doorway long before it was mine. Ed says one of two things whenever I come in or out: "Seen any good ciggy-butts lately?" or, "It's all quiet here, missy, on this side."

I stand among the sixty-three lamps in my studio, none of which is lit. I've been experimenting lately with strings of tiny white Christmas lights inside my shades, rather than the single bright bulb. I wrap the string up and down and side to side inside the lamp's wire latticework. But the little lights are cheaply made, or maybe there's a short. One tiny bulb bleeps out, and the whole thing goes. Then I have to unwind it, locate the culprit. All day long one of these strands has given me grief. I can't find the bad bulb. I think I have, and the lights come on, the paper shade shimmering with silver threads, and then the lights flicker and quit.

I'm long overdue for a trip to Sante Fe. Down there the air is clean, bright, and soft. So are the interiors of the adobe homes and the faces behind the boutique windows. When I arrive in the Albuquerque airport I'll load my crates of lamps onto a dolly. I'll brush aside the gallery van-driver's help. I like to do the work myself. The boxes are huge but not heavy. I pile them high. Boxes of lamps for the well-lit people. More light, they want. More light.

When Russell arrives in my dark studio, he says nothing for a long time. We stare down at the city, its lights flung out in unkempt rows. Far off, the airport beacon signals erratically, casting smoldering auras into the black fizz of the sky. Sleet pings off my windows.

After a while I tell him about my day. I mention the problem lamp. "It's nothing," I say. "I'm just going to toss it and go on to the next one. I've got a million more in the hopper, ready to go." I touch my temple, smile.

Wind rattles the windows' old glass. When I shiver, Russell, behind me now, puts his arms around me, crossing them over my chest. He slides his palms across my biceps. The sides of his hands brush against my breasts. When he puts his lips on the back of my neck, I lay my head against his chest, feel his warm lips as they press my throat.

"You're not telling me to stop," he whispers, and I shake my head.

When he turns me and kisses me, his kiss is not about good-bye. It has nothing to do with departure. I feel his shirt, damp from the rain. His chest, when I've undone the buttons, is cool.

Only once as we are making love do I think of his infant body slipping out, wet and bloody, into my hands.

When I think this, I bury my face in his shoulder, as if I'm Eve, going backwards, trying to reenter the ribs of her mate, becoming no one again. The baby's chest was between my two hands, the sweet pure heart already beating wildly.

"Gen," is all he says as he holds me. "Gen, Gen, Gen."

Later, when I get up, I hear him. He's on the other side of the paper screen that's my bedroom wall. I peek around it and see him squatting, naked, by the broken lamp. He's pulled out the string of little lights and is fingering the bulbs, one by one. He peers inside the sockets. Then he plugs the cord in. The lights flicker and go out. He's got the cord wrapped around his shoulders, up one arm and down the other, to keep it straight, I suppose. He fiddles with a bulb. Sleepy and still dazed by the force of his passion, I stand there watching. He plugs in the cord again, and this time the lights stay on, so brightly I can no longer see Russell. He is all light. Then the lights move toward me, laughing. They call my name.

THE EXPECTATION OF ABUNDANCE
(Connie)

Ninety thousand tons of steel
out of control—
she's more a roller coaster
than the train I used to know.

My sister Mona and her two new friends, my old ones, Scooter and Don, were singing along with the ancient record player. A baby-blue box, it gave off heat and a little hum when you got up close. The three of them were stitching leather soles onto sandals—Mona with her hair cut short like a boy's, Don with a cigarette hanging out of his mouth, and Scooter tapping his toes. All the songs they liked were about leaving—wild trains and fast cars—but nobody around here ever went anywhere.

Mona reached over and lifted the cigarette from Don's mouth, took a deep drag, winked at me where I stood in the lodge doorway, and put the cigarette back in Don's mouth.

Don didn't seem to notice. He turned the sandal over, looped a lace into a knot.

Mona called Scooter and Don the Good Old Boys, the GOBs. When I wouldn't buy her a pack of Salems, she just shrugged: "The hell with you then, the GOBs will get me one."

"You should cut down on the nicotine," I kept telling her. "It just makes you tense."

"I can only quit one thing at a time, Connie." She'd glare at me, her face flushed.

Mona had lost her yellow pallor. Considering how angry she was about her circumstances, and as bad as they obviously seemed to her—being stuck here in close quarters with me and a bunch of old hippies at the Farm—I thought she looked good. Certainly better than a month ago. No more bags under her eyes. No rashes on the insides of her arms. Last month, when she'd first stepped into my house, an old stone structure that had once served as the Farm's chicken coop, she'd stared down at her shoes in the dirt. "Connie, what *is* this? Where's the floor?" Her voice shook. Her hands trembled at her sides. She'd been off the pain-killers for only one day. "Dad would turn over in his grave if he could see how you're living."

I cleared off a ledge for Mona to sleep on, on the wall opposite mine. We each had three lawn-chair cushions that served as mattresses on our ledges. Going to sleep meant putting oneself away for the night on a shelf, an old timber plank where twenty years ago hens laid speckled eggs in the dark.

The last time I'd seen my sister, she'd been visiting me at the lab where I used to work. She had no idea how to act around the chimps—but that, as she grumbled, was not her fault. "You could have clued me in," she said. "You could have told me."

"I wasn't supposed to, Mona," I'd explained. "You were part of the experiment."

At the primate center in St. Paul, I'd ushered Mona and five other visitors into a glass-enclosed viewing area. On the other side of the glass the three chimps were napping under their willow. "Ooo, isn't that little one darling?" an older woman had said right off, stepping up to the glass and tapping it with her diamond ring.

The chimps' eyes blinked open. The male, Gregor, stood up, stretched once, sneered at the onlookers, and took off running, at first on all fours, then on just his hind legs. He hurled himself at the glass.

Mona and the others jumped back. Then they laughed, giggled really, showing gums, baring teeth.

That wasn't good.

From my bench in back I took notes on what the visitors did, what the chimps did. *Gregor banged fists four times on glass wall. Pressed tongue against glass. Drummed chest.* His black eyes were burning, radiant.

The visitors smiled and pointed to the two females

who sat huddled close together under the willow. The visitors grinned and waved to Gregor.

He turned and ran up the fake tree's trunk and swung down from a fire hose. He hated them. He was furious, but he'd get over it.

"You could have told me, Sis," Mona said later in my apartment. "You didn't have to let me go in there and be an idiot among idiots."

"Yes I did. It was my job."

Shelly, another graduate student, and I were studying the effects of "trained" versus "untrained" visitors on the chimps. We wanted to see what would happen if we gave visitors a few brief chimp etiquette lessons before we took them into the viewing area. No smiling, for instance. Chimps see the display of teeth as a sign of aggression. Or, lower your head and hold out a limp wrist to show them you consider yourself a humble guest in their territory, that you mean them no harm, that you won't be staying long.

As it turned out, even the clued-in people were embarrassing. Exaggeratedly meek. Shoulders slumped. Wrists dangling. The chimps hissed and snarled at them too.

"It's stupid anyhow," I told Mona. "We're seeing no discernible difference in the chimps' responses. They hold all strangers equally in contempt."

"Good," Mona said. "Good for them."

"I want to go down slow," Mona sang now, along with the record. Don smiled, flashing his black teeth: two on the

top right and two on the bottom left. It gave him an odd symmetry. Last night Mona had cut her own hair, using the same big black-handled scissors used to cut sandal soles from sheets of leather. Wearing a pair of my bib overalls, she had stood at the lodge house bathroom mirror, cutting. The reddish blond strands floated down around her feet. I'd been working at a table just outside the bathroom door, addressing shipping boxes for the sandals, and I'd heard her going through the cupboards, slamming doors. "Christ, I'm a prisoner. A prisoner in health-food hell," she was muttering. "Not even an ounce of NyQuil in this freakin' place." Outside, a wind howled. Then I heard the scissors.

When Mona was born she was so small our parents took turns sleeping on a cot in the kitchen to be near her. They'd brought her home from the Grand Forks hospital in a cardboard box, the one my father's dress boots had come in, those black boots with tooled laurel wreaths he'd worn to the grave. All that February after her birth, Mona, covered with sheep's wool and gray flannel, slept in that box, which sat on the stove's propped-open oven door.

"She's so red," I'd say, peering in, the oven's low heat warming my own face. I was four.

My mother would pull the flannel over Mona's tiny fists, which kept escaping, flailing against the warm air.

"She looks plenty hot," I'd tell my mother.

"No, she's fine, Connie. She's just little. The doctor says if she makes it to March, she'll be home free."

But some mornings when the whole bottom of

Mona's face pulled in and her mouth opened, her scream seemed to circle through the oven's black emptiness, gaining force in there, then echoing back out—wild and high like a trapped animal's.

I stuck the last label on the last sandal box and stuck my head in the bathroom door.

Mona pulled up a hunk of hair and snipped it off.

"We have someone up the road—Pauline, remember her?—who cuts hair really well," I said.

She scowled at me in the mirror and clipped off another hunk. "I'm doing just fine, Con. Believe it or not."

"You look good in those overalls," was all I could think to say. "You may as well keep them."

*   *   *

"Fuck this," Mona said to the black clouds rolling down from Canada later that night. Her hands shook. "I can't imagine what you people do out here in the winter." She turned from the window and climbed up onto her shelf. When I handed her another blanket, I saw that her wrists were swollen and red; a few fingers were permanently bent at odd angles. Her disease, lupus, had begun coursing again, savage and poisonous.

"How about some hot tea?" I asked her.

"That camel-piss?"

"Chamomile."

Pathetic. I could see her thinking it. She rolled her eyes. "Are there any other choices?"

When our mother had called last month from Chicago in the middle of the night, she was sure the dealers—*pushers*, she called them—were about to put out a hit on Mona. Her voice was shrill, breathless. She'd left a box of Great-Grandmother Clara's china on the front stoop and told the men to come get it and never bother her again. And although neither she nor Mona had heard a car out front, or even a single noise on the porch step, the box had disappeared. Those dishes, Mother kept saying between sobs, were worth every bit of the $1,800 of Mona's debt.

Then the men began calling again. That's when Mother sold off two of Dad's "art" pieces and bought my sister a plane ticket. We all agreed the object was to get Mona the hell out of Chicago.

"A man gave me two hundred dollars for that one of the Indian princess feeding the eagle. Remember it?" my mother had asked me.

I squinted, trying to recall the piece of intricately cut paper. I could see my father himself quite clearly, sitting up late at the kitchen table, turning the crisp paper and snipping. It was an art called *scherenschnitte*, which he'd learned as a boy from his father. The small scissors seemed even smaller in his long heavy fingers, the same fingers that, come sunup, would squeeze and pull on our cows' teats.

"Here"—I reached toward Mona's feet on the ledge— "let me rub your ankles."

She threw the blanket over them. "Rubbing sucks."

"There's a bottle of raspberry wine," I said, ". . . somewhere."

She flopped onto her side. "Sure, turn me into a wino. Now that's *really* the bottom of the dunghill."

"I know I'm not much help, Mona. I can't even imagine—"

"That's right. You *can't.* Your life is sweet." She stared over my head toward the door, which sat crooked on its hinges and wouldn't close snugly. The wind howled through cracks on either side.

What her lupus doctors had first prescribed for her pain, back when she was just fifteen, and then, after she'd begun to cry on the phone for more and they'd cut her off, and what later, through her early twenties, the black market dealers had sold to her—everything to erase the pain—was gone now. I offered carrot loaf, herb tea, goat cheese.

Pathetic.

"Then tell me, Mona. Try."

She stared at the ceiling. "You don't even know you're in love with it. That's the joke, see. Until you try to break up with it."

"Do you think it's over now?

"Connie, Connie, Connie." She sighed.

"Maybe almost?"

The ends of her hair were ragged, her bangs uneven. But somehow, as she turned and shook her head at me, the haircut suited her. "Everyone thinks it's about pleasure. Untrue. You're plugging along in a blah-life in a blah-body, and pop—*voilà*—you're outside all that. You've been picked up and shot clear of the *blah*. Are you reading me?"

I nodded.

"Everywhere you step or turn, it hurts. Or, at best, it's just blah blah blah, and then"—she snapped her fingers—"you're somewhere else. You're out of it."

Later, after I had put myself atop my shelf for the night, I made myself drift away, in my own manner, casting my thoughts back toward a huge green lady, that statue I'd climbed as a child with my father. Lady Liberty, he'd called her. I held his hand and we went up the steep narrow steps beneath her bronze skirts. He'd pointed to her huge iron I-beams, wanting me to see the welds and ingenuously designed steel scaffolding.

Mother had stayed outside and down below with Mona, who, no matter how firmly Dad had pleaded, would-n't budge. She held her thin arms rigidly at her sides. She wore new white leather shoes and a red kerchief, the kind old ladies from the Old Country wore. She shook her head, her tears falling, though she wasn't making a sound.

"She's too little, I guess," my mother said, looking directly at her.

My father scowled. He took Mona's chin in his palm and tipped her face up to his. "Can't you be big? We came a long way. Be brave now."

Mona scowled at him, her eyes shimmering, wet and aloof. Her red scarf had slipped half off her head.

Dad turned and looked toward the water, the great

Atlantic. "It was raining when we came up through the Verrazano Narrows," he said, and we all knew he'd slipped back into his boyhood again, standing on the boat as it arrived. His family were Germans who'd immigrated to Russia and lived along the Volga River until the Russians tried to draft them into their wars. "The lady seemed to be coming right at us," he was saying softly. "Magnificent. As if she walked on the waves."

"Where was I?" I asked my mother.

"You. You were nowhere, Connie. Not even a thought yet in anyone's mind." She bent to straighten Mona's scarf, and Mona stopped crying and put her little finger, red and raw from so much sucking, into her mouth.

Later that day in Battery Park my father hurried us around a corner. Taxis honked loudly, calling our attention in all directions at once. "Don't look, girls," my father said. But it was too late. I'd already seen: a man by the curb, peeing against it. I saw the stream arc, heard its hiss.

"Why's that man doing that?" I asked my father.

"Because he's sad." He pulled me forward by my arm. "He's in America and he has no god. That's why. He has only one very big sadness. What it is I do not know. So don't ask me, Connie. Don't."

Inside the enormous lady, a person looks and looks away. So many bolts and rivets. The hundred mysterious languages of her visitors bubble and growl like gastronomical juices along her belly joists. My father's guttural German mingles with the low vowels from men in turbans, and with the music murmured by women in veils, by girls in layers of silk.

I climb the statue's steps that pivot and whirl. Mona is a tiny red-headed bug down below by the statue's foot. And I'm high up, entangled among the struts and the many climbers huffing their way to the top. Our laughter echoes back at the echoed laughter. We follow only our boot soles up, and no one can distinguish which voice goes with which face. Higher and higher, around the big girders. Someone's counting, but in a language I don't know. The 168 stairs criss-cross the cross-braces. We touch the underside of the lady's copper petticoats. For a fee she is open to all. Pay the ferryman and he'll carry you across the black waters.

*   *   *

"I guess you're going to make me go outside to smoke this," Mona said the next morning, pulling a cigarette from behind her ear.

I blinked, leaned toward her, and peered at the cigarette. She was still in her nightgown and fuzzy blue slippers.

"Relax, Connie, it's only tobacco. The Good Old Boys gave me a pack."

I got up and watched her through the window as she brushed wood chips off the chopping block and sat down on it. When she put her head back to inhale, a sweet look spread over her face. Propped against the stump, the ax head lay by her slippered feet, and as she smoked, she ran a finger along its blade. Across the road, the forest stretched into what seemed an infinite and impenetrable blackness. All through October Mona and I had watched wild creatures step tentatively out of it—deer, elk, cougar, and two brown bear cubs who'd nibbled once from my sweetpea vines and run back into the trees. "Hurry," Mona'd shout when she saw anything, even the young white-tailed deer I barely noticed anymore. "Hurry, Sis. Come quick." I'd stand beside her at the window and we'd watch some creature sniff the air, looking cautiously about. "He's checking the place out," Mona'd say, "and he's not too sure."

I was fond of the animals, too. Six years ago, when I'd been just ten credits away from a Ph.D. in animal behavioral sciences, I'd decided to spend a summer in northeastern Washington, where summers were reputedly mild. I was supposed to conduct a field study at Curtain Creek Farm and bring back a paper on communal child-rearing and early language acquisition. We thought we might see crossovers to ways the baby chimps back in St. Paul were learning words.

Using American Sign Language, baby chimps could say YOU ME HIDE, which meant you were supposed to toss a blanket over their heads and wait for them to yank it back off—your basic peek-a-boo. They couldn't get enough of it.

The babies at the Farm sat in plastic wading pools. The dogs licked their faces and the babies laughed. I wrote down *ga-ga* and *patty-cake* and I took sticks out of the babies' mouths, sticks the dogs had dropped in the pool. I had twenty-five pages of investigative topics: the pecking order of toddlers, aggressive versus nonaggressive games . . . But the babies were boring, devoid of that strange otherness the chimps had so much of.

Shelly sent me photos from St. Paul: the year-old chimp we'd named Rikka clowning in a big floppy hat, watching herself in the mirror, holding her pet kitten over the toilet. On the back of that one Shelly had written, *Teaching kitty to flush.*

Rikka's brother Gus had been sent to a Phoenix lab where they shot him up with HIV. The mother had died of hepatitis C in a Dallas lab. The father chimp, Ernie, had apparently risen above it all: orbiting in outer space. Once a week we'd see his face beamed back on the lab's closed-circuit TV. "LOOK," we'd sign to Rikka, "THERE'S YOUR DAD."

"DEAD," Rikka would sign with one emphatically flipped palm.

"NO, SLEEPING," Shelly would tell her.

Then Rikka would go up close to the TV, peering at Ernie's grizzled face. Once, she'd try to feed him her banana, tried to push it through the wire mesh over the TV screen. Then she'd smacked the wire and turned to us. Shelly and I, watching old Ernie in a cloud of interstellar static, smiled weakly. We didn't know then that little Rikka was right about her father. Although the other scientists knew, Shelly and I wouldn't find out for another month that yes, Ernie was indeed a corpse circling high over everyone's heads.

"THREE O'CLOCK," Rikka signed and pointed to the wall clock. "CARTOON. CARTOON." She wanted the other channel now: *Rocky and Bullwinkle.*

For knowledge, says Lao-Tze, add something every day; for wisdom, take something away. What we were doing with the chimps was not for them. It was for the experimenters. That's what I'd finally come to understand at Curtain Creek. Beyond our small world there, more and more knowledge in the big world kept getting added on, and nothing was ever taken away.

In the Farm's plastic pool the babies cooed a familiar babble. The Farm's babies were dull, but unexpectedly, the grownups weren't. They had a thousand causes to support. Landfills to close. Police brutality to protest. A man had died in the Spokane County Jail, strapped too tightly all night inside a straitjacket. It came out in the coroner's report that he'd suffocated. Someone had to say something. Someone had to protest. That was them. That was us. We carried our placards and marched around the jail.

Still, I often missed little Rikka. I'd brought her that tiger-striped kitten in the photo. She liked to cradle it in her arms just as she'd been cradled. She named the kitten BABY, signing its name. "BABY, LOOK." She'd hold it up close to the TV screen, signing like a pro with her free hand. "SEE. FATHER DEAD. BABY SEE." The kitten mewed loudly, and Rikka, lowering the kitten into the crook of her elbow, would look up at me, sad and unsure of how to handle its distress.

*   *   *

"Someone's singing," I heard Mona say in her sleep. She lay on her shelf across the room, one arm over her head, her blankets kicked off. It was early November, and we'd both worked hard all day, pruning, raking, and burning slash. I slid down from my shelf and picked up Mona's blanket from where it had slipped to the dirt floor. Her eyelids fluttered in a line of moonlight from the window.

Who? I wanted to ask her in her dream. *Who's* singing?

That morning for breakfast, before our big day of work, Mona had made pancakes and sprinkled on huckleberries after she'd flipped the cakes once. Her technique was definitely neater than mine. A few nights before she'd made pasta with the last tomatoes and basil from the garden. She was becoming a good cook—unlike me, who never took time, never opened a recipe book.

"Hotcakes stay with you all day long," I said in a singsong voice. "That's what we say out here." I held up a forkful like a little flag.

Mona was chewing bubble gum, her new stop-smoking aid, and she poured more batter onto the griddle. "*Hotcakes.* So is that a Northwest word? All's we know in Chicago is *pancakes.*" She lifted two more onto my plate. In the last couple of weeks she'd been talking about getting her own apartment soon, and a dog, maybe, a little Shih Tzu. "They don't bark much," she said, "or jump all over you like the wild mongrels out here."

Later we scanned the Farm's fall chore list, which had been pushed under our door the night before. "I can't cut limbs off trees," Mona said, "but I can do *something.*"

"You could tend the fire," I said.

Mona snapped her gum. "And just what does that entail?"

I explained about the pitchfork and the hose and how to keep the flames low. "A controlled burn. That's the basic idea."

"Got it," she said.

By late afternoon we were all working in thick clouds of billowing smoke. "Just let her do it *her* way," I kept telling the others. But Mona's way was to heap the brush and limbs onto the burn pile in bigger and bigger quantities until orange flames shot up brightly. I took her a dozen wheelbarrow loads of pine needles, which she hoisted quickly onto the fire with the pitchfork. Her short hair was a mess of twigs and ash, her right elbow bound up in a filthy Ace bandage, but she was smiling.

Everyone lugged limbs out to her, setting them at her feet, and she'd bend and carefully select one, then heave it on the pile. Her eyes were glassy from the smoke. All day we hiked back and forth from Mona's burn pile as if it were the hub, the hot sun, of our tiny universe.

And that night, as I'd pulled the blanket back over her, I'd felt a little jab of déjà vu. We were girls again. She'd kicked off her covers and wanted me to look inside her closet for monsters.

"They're gone, Mona."

"Look. *Please.*"

I got out of my bed and opened the closet door. "Nope. Not a single one." I closed the door again.

Our father also used to call out in his sleep. He'd shout something in German, a profanity, Mona and I thought, listening in the hallway—a word no doubt aimed at that Russian general who'd burned their village church in the Volga River Valley.

As he himself would say, our father was not a man of consequence. He'd run a dairy farm on eighty dry acres of North Dakota clay, scratching at the parched red earth, coaxing up slim shoots of hay. He believed if he treated the cows well, they would give and give, and that if the earth were tilled during the right phase of the moon, it would heap its bounties upon us. Whole summers of drought didn't diminish his faith. I'd pass his door at night and see him on his knees by his bed, hands clasped, whispering in German just as, years earlier, I'd seen him pray over that tiny red infant chirping like a baby bird in her bootbox on the open oven door.

*   *   *

Mona had been smoking again. Not tobacco this time, but the Good Old Boys' homegrown grass. Don, Scooter, and Mona were sewing sandals and singing along to the music, which was so loud it seemed to shut out whatever didn't issue forth from right down inside it—a guitar in pure misery, a saxophone commiserating. Outside the lodge, the first November snows were falling, quiet and gentle.

My sister and the boys were laughing. She had tan laces in her hand. Her face was close to the leather sandal sole as she peered at the awl holes, then poked the needle in. All the while her lips silently mouthed the lyrics—another song about a train, this one hurtling through Texas or Tennessee, states none of us had ever set foot in.

Don lowered his head and glanced at her stitches. He smiled. The black teeth looked like tiny keyholes in his mouth. The grass smelled musty, pungent, barely dry enough to smoke.

"Can you turn that music any higher?" I called from the lodge doorway.

Mona raised her sewing needle. "We're as high as we go," she said. "Hey, kill that mouse up there, would you, Sis?" Mona jerked her head toward the window directly opposite their work table. "These guys *won't*."

"Like I told you," Scooter said, "that mouse lives here, Mona."

I glanced up at the plump little gray fellow happily washing his tiny paws atop the windowsill.

Mona made a knot at her sandal's heel. "Ha. You said the same thing about those black widows in the shower stall."

Don handed her another lace. "Look," he said, "everything's copacetic here. We're all just fending for ourselves."

I took a deep breath, trying to let my anger go but feeling it settle instead, low in my chest. For two days I'd been in Olympia talking to people at the Department of Fish and Wildlife. The men were sick of cleaning up the geese's thin gray scat from the state parks, and they were proposing to kill off thousands of Canada geese. They'd convinced a few legislators that this was a good idea; the meat would all go to food banks. I'd knocked on shiny oak doors, trying to stop the slaughter. I'd mentioned that maybe we should think about why the geese were so fond of our parks in the first place. Maybe if we just stopped feeding them hot dog buns and potato chips, they'd go on up north.

The song was suddenly over, and the needle went *scree-scree*ing over the antiquated black vinyl. The quiet blasted around us.

"Hey, where'd the tunes go?" Scooter looked up at me. "Turn the record over, would you, Connie?"

I walked across the room and stood in front of them at their work table. "I thought I told you guys, Mona's trying to quit the mind-alterations."

"Why?" Scooter's voice boomed as if the music were still playing.

All three of them, Mona too, stared up at me, their hands pausing in mid-stitch.

"She's trying to go straight," I said.

"I'm only a little bent," Mona whispered. "So are *they*."

Don smiled. "Maybe straight's not as great as it's cracked up to be, Connie."

"That's right," Mona said. "I've been there."

I frowned at Mona. "No you *haven't*." I touched my fingertips to the top of their work table. I could see then what I was to them. A downer. A splash of cold water in their warm faces.

"Yeah, I have," Mona said. "A long time ago. I give it a seventy-six. It's got an okay lyric, but you can't dance to it."

"Hey, we're working here, Sister," Don said. "Now that

we've gotten ourselves online, we're getting orders every day, not to mention all these that keep dribbling in from the mail." He patted a handful of envelopes. "Are you going to flip that record or what?"

Scooter picked up a pile of leather soles, held them out to me, shook them gently, and let them drop. "Look, Connie, we've got miles to go before we sleep."

I shook my head at the three of them. It was too late anyway to change a single thing about what had already happened here. I was tired. I had to let it go. And who was I, anyway, to say? Who the hell was *I?*

I turned and walked across the room to the little blue record player. Someone had taped a pen on its fat black arm to keep the needle from jumping out of the groove. As I turned the record over, I could see the scratches and smudges made by the dirty hands of a hundred strangers who'd passed a little time among us. The needle went down, and a bass guitar twanged. This made Mona and the GOBs smile again, and made me stand there a moment and close my eyes.

*   *   *

Around Thanksgiving, I came home from another Olympia trip to find my few pieces of furniture outside on the grass. Mona was sitting on the couch, smoking who knew what. Scooter and Don, covered with a paste-colored dust, were stretched out on the ground. The weather had taken a sudden warm turn, and the sun was bright.

The three of them sat up when they saw me. Mona

patted a place on the couch next to her. "Take a load off, Sis. You look wasted."

I dropped my satchel on the couch and headed for the house.

"Hold on now, Connie," Don called. "You can't go in there yet."

I turned and glared at Mona. "What is this?"

Mona just smiled and blew out a cloud of smoke.

"The floor's not dry yet," Scooter said, "but you can look."

"Just one peek," Mona called.

I pulled open my door and was surprised when it swung out toward me, soundlessly clearing the stoop. Scooter and Don had evidently fixed it, shaved off a bit on the bottom, and rehung it. I stuck my head inside. There was a floor now. They'd poured a slab of concrete and troweled it smooth.

"You couldn't keep on like that, Connie," Mona called from the couch. "You'd have bugs all winter. Those killer spiders."

The damp floor glistened. I turned and looked at them. I gave them a little bow. "Thank you," I said. "Thank you all."

"It's practically a real house now," Mona said. "Hey, did you save those geeses yet?"

"Nope," I said. "There're many miles to go."

Outside, that night, with Mona on the couch, and me on a rug on the ground, we watched clouds swirl around the stars. I had no idea then that I'd already planted one foot squarely inside my future. By this time the next year, I'd be carrying a briefcase; I'd have a column in a nature magazine. On our newly hooked-up computer in the lodge, I'd send faxes and e-mail about the animals I was trying to save.

But that night under the stars, Mona and I lay there talking about the past; about Dad's cows—his girls, he used to call them. A few days after the third stroke, the one that finally took him, we'd watched from the back porch as our neighbor Mr. Olmstead hauled the cows away in his truck.

"Oh god, didn't they bellow?" Mona asked. "I'll remember that sound as long as I live."

"It was awful," I said, recalling how the low wails sailed out at us. From the truck, the cows' heads turned toward us, and their black eyes found our faces.

I'd been away from the lab for ten days for Dad's funeral, and when I returned, the chimps had to be restrained from hugging me. A hug from a grown chimp—and ours were growing!—could crush a person's ribs. WHERE CONNIE? Rikka asked me, meaning where had I been. I signed to her about my father dying. Rikka turned to Shelly. PLEASE, Rikka signed to her, PLEASE CONNIE HUG.

It had been snowing heavily that day, and the chimps stood at the window, their noses pressed to the glass like first-graders kept inside at recess. As their playground filled with snow, we kept signing the same thing. NO. TOO COLD. NO GO OUTSIDE. We fed them strawberry yogurt and cans of Pepsi. Suddenly Gregor turned from the glass, signing frantically to us: COATS, he said. BRING COATS.

Trying to drift into sleep under the stars, I aimed myself due east, to the usual place. I propelled myself up there on the balcony around the green lady's torch. There, I'm a tenth the size of her fingernail. I've climbed up the swirled vein in her arm and watched the door in her wrist swing open, so I can finally step out and stand in the light of her hundred dazzling bulbs.

Manhattan slips off into a mesh of gold bangles: flickering, wet, floating. My father and I and the few climbers who've made it are winded, dizzy, and proud of our endurance. What we have for no one else, we have for the lady. We're wild for her. She offers us, like gumdrops on her palm, to the clouds; her island's a lily pad at her feet. The city that long ago emerged to bow down to her now backs away. It curtsies and disappears from the horizon's edge. And we're up there. We soar above the stars in her crown.

Sometimes even now, five years after Mona's move to Tempe, I remember her as she was that day when she helped me set the furniture back inside the house and spread the rug on the new concrete floor. We'd just settled everything neatly into place when the first of many snow storms that winter began. We watched it come down in thick sheets. Mona helped me chop vegetables for stew, and she talked again of moving to Tempe in the spring. She imagined a little apartment—stucco, she said, very clean, with a big air conditioner. She'd heard the dry air in Arizona was easier on people with her disease.

I was slicing carrots over the stew pot with a tiny paring knife, one at a time.

"Connie, why make it so hard on yourself? Use a real knife." Mona produced a cleaver. I watched her line up six carrots on the bread board. "Okay, watch this now. It's all in the wrist." And precise and quick as any electric chopping gadget, she smacked across all the carrots at once, leaving six neat rows of slices.

Later, with our stew simmering, she put on my snowboots and stepped outside. But when I looked out the window for her, she wasn't there. Then I heard her. Up on the roof. She'd found the snow shovel and was going at it. I pulled a blanket around myself and stepped out.

"Hey," I called, "hey, take it easy up there."

Big snowflakes were falling on her shoulders. "Sis, you have to keep a stupid flat roof like this shoveled good. Or it'll leak."

"I know," I said, "but just don't get cold. Come in soon."

She gave a thumbs up to the sky.

By March she had moved to Tempe. She lived a year there, holding down a good job keeping medical records in a hospital. Then she slipped. She was in and out of rehab for four years. She kept trying to survive. She'd haul herself out of bed with her huge knuckles and fat, swollen ankles. She'd aim the curling iron through what the lupus drugs had left her of her hair and dab on her lavender eye shadow—until, on one hot August day, her kidneys finally shut down.

In her tiny basement apartment my mother and I found the lists she'd made, so dizzy on black-market morphine she'd had to remind herself to "shave legs, plug in curling iron, make coffee, eat toast, don't forget purse."

That first blizzardy day at the Farm, watching her up on the roof, the big white flakes brushing her cheeks, I'd been afraid she'd slip. Years of cortisone had left her bones brittle. Watch out, I kept thinking; don't stumble, don't fall. Her face was flushed the color of the red dogwoods down by the creek. I just shook my head, smiling, as I shake it now, remembering. Mona lowered her shovel and lifted it again, heavy with snow. One after another, she cut enormous slices out of the snow and then tossed them easily away.

TREAT ME NICE

(Francine)

The night was a sieve of money. Everyone held out cupped palms. Under the steaming casino lights, roulette wheels and slot machines whooped it up. On the main stage Sergio "The Surge" Raz and Duncan Farrow had finally finished their Boxomania match. Duncan Farrow had lost, but no matter. He still got a big pot: five percent of the door's take, in a blue plastic bag. His left eye was swollen shut, his lip cut, but he was smiling. He carried the blue bag by its plastic grips, passing among the summer tourists, all drunk, who had driven up from Spokane and Coeur d'Alene to the Triple Eagle Casino, and who soon—after we'd voted for an Elvis of the Evening—would swagger back to their Buicks and veer south to the lowlands.

My mother had heard a radio ad about the International Elvis Invitational, and all week she hadn't shut up about it. "Elvis, he's my man," she kept saying. "He's the one."

"All right already," I said when I couldn't take any more. "But you'll have to be good. All the way 'til Friday."

We went over the list. She wasn't to touch the kitchen stove while I was at work. No frying coffee grounds and Corn Chex in a skillet. No bringing rocks indoors. And no hiding any of my clothes—socks, underwear, my nurses' aide uniforms, nothing!—in the crawlspace under the house.

"Of course not, Francine. I wouldn't dream of it."

Glancing at myself in the window during one of these discussions—my right hand on my hip, my face stern—I saw *her*. Scolding. *You're not going anywhere, young lady, without your shoes. Who do you think you are?*

And "Who are *you?*" she'll ask me sometimes in the mornings. But before I've swallowed my coffee to speak, she'll have answered the question. "Oh yes. I know. I remember. Francine Lennertz."

"Your daughter."

"Of course you are." Shaking her head gently, as if I were the one confused.

After the boxing ring was dismantled and the blood mopped off the stage by two teenage girls—"not even wearing gloves," I muttered to my mother—the Elvis impersonators came on.

My mother took a sip of my gin. She'd been sneaking sips all night, but now she was past being sly. I kept ordering. One more—I'd hold up a finger to Ann Marie, the waitress, who wore a tiny diamond in her nose. She'd lived with us for a few months on the Farm. Back then, her head had been shaved and her skull tattooed with a turquoise snake. I knew she wasn't twenty-one, but the Triple Eagle wasn't exactly known for its law-abidingness. One more, I'd said to her three or four times. It was impossible to keep track of how much gin had gone into me, and how much into my mother.

Up on stage when the Elvises ground their groins, my mother put her hands over her eyes and peeked through her fingers. There was the Sikh Elvis in a turban and thick dark beard. An emaciated Elvis. An old, humped, arthritic-spined Elvis. A Russian Elvis with a gray ponytail and Lenin's face emblazoned on his huge silver belt buckle. Elvis in a yarmulke. Elvis in a cowboy hat.

And my mother's voice, loud over "Jailhouse Rock," directed at Ann Marie who'd come bearing my drink: "I'm more with it than I seem, honey. Don't let these bugged-out eyes fool you."

I sat back and sipped. My ankles were puffy from the day's walking—up and down the antiseptic-smelling corridors of St. Boniface Hospital. I rode out of the fog-filled canyon to ply my trade, or as some of my neighbors would say, my collusion with the powers of commerce.

The boxer, Duncan Farrow, whose bottom I'd bathed last year when he was lying on the third floor, my floor, with his leg in traction, stopped by our table and held up his blue plastic bag. My mother smiled at it, nodded. He kept asking people to call him The Pharaoh, but no one did. He'd grown up down the road from the casino, and we'd all known him when he was just a scruffy kid. He leaned close to me. "What do you think, Francine?" He touched his lip. "Is this going to need stitches?"

"I'm not allowed to give medical advice," I said. "I'm just an aide." I shook my head. "But put something on that."

Ann Marie handed him a small glass, and he quickly tossed back its amber liquid. "How's that?"

The crowd at the next table laughed. Ann Marie touched Duncan's shoulder. She wore her hair in a pageboy now. I smiled at her, thinking about the snake I knew lay coiled and concealed beneath her dark hair. Duncan slipped an arm around her waist.

When the six-year-old Elvis in blue suede shoes ran gleefully on stage, "Awww," was the exhaled sigh that rose through the room. My mother looked from the boy in his rhinestone-studded shirt to me, and her eyes welled with tears. "Oh, Francine," she said, "isn't he dear?"

But don't you, the boy belted out, *don't you step on my blue suede shoes.* We had a ringside table. An hour ago, during the boxing, we'd seen bubbles of blood fly from Duncan's mouth—the mouth that was smiling now since someone had just passed him another shot.

When it was all sung and done, we'd have to vote. My mother dabbed her eyes. She'd been good all week. She'd sat in the gold recliner, cranking up and down the radio dial, talking on the phone to her friend Edna who was just as far gone as she was, but who lived in the home for the far-gones in Kettle Falls.

"Hand me your napkin, honey," my mother said. Two tears, one from each eye, dripped down her cheeks. The boy's shoes, kicking up, were sky-blue.

The next Elvis made the ladies squeal. He was the fifties heartthrob. Not the sixties mover-groover, not the seventies Vegas mainstay. This Elvis slowed down the air in the Triple Eagle. *Love me tender*, he sang, and amazingly, his face did not contort. I felt his calm, felt the muscles in my legs relax.

Halfway through his song, two women staggered up, leaned across the stage, and reached over the red footlights to touch his black jeans. He nodded to them, sidestepping their hands. He was trying to maintain his composure, I thought, even as he maneuvered over the microphone cord in a way that suggested he believed this whole thing was silly—and that made him just a crazy bit real.

Never let me go, he sang. The two women, clearly blasted, had gotten their hands on the microphone cord, and suddenly they yanked. The microphone conked onto the stage, and its reverb sputtered.

The gentle Elvis, still smiling, bent to retrieve it, and, just as he did, the women grabbed his shirt. So much chaos surrounded the calm Elvis, it was bound to finally catch him. And then my name was called twice across the ruckus, "Francie, Francie," followed by my mother's usual cry of distress: "Oh golly, oh golly." There was a yelp and a scuffle of jeans as Elvis flipped over our heads.

"Oh Francie," a whimpering voice was saying. "Oh golly. Here he comes."

*　　*　　*

In St. Bonnie's two weeks later, the calm Elvis, whose name was Perry, was worse, not better. It wasn't the gash on his leg that kept him here, but a wound infection that was baffling to the staff. I'd bathe him and change his sheets at the same time. It's the hospital system. I'd turn him on one hip, swab his backside, roll the old sheets out and shove the new ones under, then turn him, gently, across the linen, and pull loose the old sheets, which were warm, very warm, from his fever. Then I'd smooth down the new, cool ones.

In the afternoons Perry liked to tune the overhead TV to the Fulfillment Channel. Once, he'd ask me if I'd ever tried that Peach Bliss body lotion. "What with all the baths you give, I bet you could use a good hand lotion. Want me to buy it for you? Really, Francine. Pass me that phone."

"Lie back now," I told him. "You're all done." I pulled his I.V. stand up by his bed. With the penicillin drip inside, the tubing was the color of opals.

Then I took off my gloves and put my hand on his forehead. Without his Elvis wig, he had a ruddy, receding hairline. His soft brown hair, what little of it there was, he wore pulled back into a needle-thin ponytail. The nurses and orderlies kept telling me he was in love with me. Head over heels. But no, I'd say—to them, and to myself—no, he's just long gone in the Streptococcus A.

"What's up with me, sweetheart? Can you tell old Perry the truth? No one else will." He'd close his eyes. Wait for my answer. He had courage. He wanted to face facts, grim as they were.

"This new medicine is going to do the trick," I'd tell him.

Often we'd hear a *whap-whap-whap* outside. "Jerk-offs," Perry'd say when we saw the helicopter whir past his window. No doubt it was delivering yet another new doctor to the hospital. Soon he'd appear in Perry's room—to treat himself to a titillating medical intrigue, a freaky blip on the green charts.

All around the room were flowers from Elvises around the globe. Gladiolus and popcorn plants. I read him the cards. The Iranian Elvis who'd finally won that night, and whom we'd missed, wrote to offer Perry financial assistance.

"Ha! I've got a million bucks in the bank," Perry said.

Every day another doctor touched down on St. Bonnie's roof: a stranger in our far corner of Washington. I'd stand and hold Perry's hand while a doctor shuffled through his chart's pages. Maybe it was necrotizing fasciitis. Maybe it was streptococcal toxic shock syndrome. Whatever it was, the immune system had gone berserk, spewing too many inflammatory mediators, good things meant to heal. But the good mediators had turned nasty, greedy. They'd gone out of bounds, eating beyond the wound's edges.

Propped on four pillows, Perry's ankle, with what had first been a simple gash, incurred when he'd landed on a tray of glasses, was now a bulge of purple and blue blisters full of bright yellow liquid.

Tick, tick, tick was the sound the newest doctor's tongue made against his teeth. He flipped the chart's green pages.

Perry squeezed my hand. "Check her out, Francie." He

tipped his chin toward the overhead TV, where a busty red-head was oiling her cleavage with a lotion. "A bargain," claimed a voice, "at only twenty-nine ninety-five for the economical liter size."

"I'd like to do that to you," Perry whispered. "Oil you up and down."

The new doctor, dry-lipped and in need of a shave, looked at me and frowned. Then he turned to a fresh sheet on his clipboard, scribbled, stopped, and shook the pen. "Blast." He glared at me. "Doesn't anything around here work?"

*   *   *

My mother hung up the phone and stepped to the kitchen counter, scowling down at what I was grating into a bowl. "Oh my God, what *is* that? It looks like a penis." She'd asked me this a dozen times.

"Ginger root," I said.

She sighed loudly and looked past me, out the window. "Your father and I used to eat porterhouse steaks every Saturday night. Sometimes a nice ribeye." She smiled.

"Was that Edna on the phone?"

"Completely bonkers." My mother twirled her finger by her ear vigorously, reminding me of the way I'd once poked a pin into a frog's head and how stirring what was inside felt like scrambling a tiny egg.

"She's more out to lunch than I am. Much more." My mother yanked her hairbrush from her sweatshirt pocket and began brushing her hair straight back from her forehead.

"What's going to happen with that penis root?"

"It's for the tofu marinade." I added a tablespoon of garlic to the bowl, then brown sugar, wine, tamari.

As she brushed her hair, she watched me. "For the tootie fruity," she hummed. "I guess I'll never eat another hamburger in this lifetime. I've just got to accept that, don't I?" The static electricity had made a few fine white hairs around her forehead stand up.

"Mom, if you want meat, okay. No problem. I'll bring you a steak. Will that make you happy?"

"Not if I have to hear about those mad cows again. Cause if I do, it's not worth it." She bent and sniffed the tofu. "What's the news on the showstopper?" she asked without looking up. We'd been the ones to help Perry to the hospital after his topple off the stage. My mother, in a streak of lucidity, had shouted at Ann Marie to get us a clean towel. I'd pulled the shard of glass out of Perry's ankle, and my mother had passed me the towel as if I were a surgeon and she were my nurse.

"No!" my mother had snapped at the two women who'd caused all the trouble in the first place and who were still shrieking, but this time for someone to call 911. "No, we don't need an ambulance. That'll take too long. My daughter's a nurse. We'll drive this Elvis ourselves, for Christ's sake. To the sick place. All you people, get out of our way!"

*   *   *

Three weeks passed, then four. And then last week, week five, I stood with Gladys and Deedee, two of the other nurse's aides, in the bleach-stinking hallway, where we pretended not to eavesdrop on two doctors talking near the nurses' station. Gladys took out her nicotine gum and offered a cube of it to me and then to Deedee, but we just wrinkled our noses. We leaned against the cool gray walls, hearing the doctors' same lame drivel about Perry. "Boost the clindamycin in the penicillin drip."

"Yeah, yeah, yeah." Gladys said.

"Francine, you be extra careful taking those gloves off," Deedee whispered.

They both glanced at my hands, hands that only an hour ago—in gloves—had swabbed Perry's genitals, lifting the scrotum gently. "Honey pie," he'd whispered. He'd smiled a sad smile. I'd kissed his forehead, which was pale and much too warm.

"Right," Gladys echoed. "Watch yourself, Francie."

I liked them. I'd never had to say to them what I'd had to say all my life: *Hi, I'm Francine. I'm new.* Never that. "Well, Francine, thank God you're here. Finally. Can you take four-oh-four a bedpan, honey?" Those were Gladys's first words to me. She'd patted my arm. "And that's the cleanest damn uniform I've ever seen."

When I stepped back into Perry's room, he was on the phone, reading off numbers from a credit card. He'd stop and start again. He grinned and put his palm over the receiver. "A surprise for you, baby. Don't listen. Come back later."

I went to his bed and took the card out of his hand, slipped it inside his nightstand drawer.

"What's the address here? They want a number and a street." He put his head back on the pillow, his thin ponytail a wet string. "I don't even know this zip code."

I took the phone from him and hung it up. His breaths were rushed, shallow, his face flushed. "Tell me again," he said, "what's the name of this town? I want to hang those earbobs on your earlobes." His eyelids fluttered closed. "I've got a million bucks in the bank."

"Never mind now. There's nothing I need."

A short time later he was singing a few wispy breaths against my hair. ". . . burnin' love." Then he was humming, barely. And then he stopped. No melody. No music. He was all short low moans. "Darlin', darlin', darlin'," he sang. But it wasn't a song. It was a fevered love.

*   *   *

Hi. I'm Francine. I'm new. It was my mantra from childhood and teenagedom, and sometimes, even now in my mid-thirties, it came charging back to me, scooting across foggy thoughts as I woke, or as I drifted off. Twelve states: I'd lived in that many during the first eighteen years of my life. No two grades finished in the same town. The new math in New York reverted to the old math in Maine. It always began with my father telling us across those porterhouse steaks, "It's a better job. A nicer town. A bigger house." And then my mother and me crying, later, softly, in the kitchen. "He says we can't take Kitty with us," she whispers into my shoulder, her face as damp as mine. "It's too far."

The cardboard boxes used and reused. Battered and scuffed. *Hi, I'm new. I'm Francine.* The bigger houses blur. The towns are silver tacks on a map. Seen from a distance, they make the outline of a crooked dipper, the ladle of our lives, the constellation Lennertz. My mother and I out here alone now, on the tip of the handle in the Hoodoo Valley.

There's not a single thing we can do about what's coming, about the one of us who'll soon slip from the map. It won't be like my father's smooth quick exit: a leap out of the middle of a heartbeat in the middle of the night. The doctors have told us what we might expect: that my mother will probably forget how to breathe, how to swallow. The brain will let go, bit by bit, of everything a person doesn't even know she knows. She'll forget how to walk, how to smile. She'll forget daytime, nighttime, the succession of states and houses, each with the same rose-chintz curtains in the kitchen. She'll forget the tomatoes ripening on our windowsill. She'll forget a song about blue suede shoes. She'll forget singing. She'll forget you, Francine. To her, you'll be new. Go ahead then. Say it. *Hi, I'm Francine. I'm new.*

*　　*　　*

"Who is it?" Perry asked. I was standing at his window, looking out, and I turned when he spoke and motioned Duncan inside.

"The Pharaoh," Duncan said. "I was in the neighborhood."

"Who?" Perry raised up on his elbows.

"Duncan. Duncan Farrow." He sat down near the door and folded his hands tightly in his lap.

"Drunken sorrow," Perry whispered. The ridiculous red sock Gladys had stuck like a cap over his blackened toes bobbed.

Duncan glanced at the sock and then down at his own hands.

"Don't feel sorry, boy," Perry said. "It's not sad. It's just weird."

"I had to get a half dozen stitches cut loose." Duncan touched his lip.

"Didn't you win yourself a pile of money?" Perry asked him.

The boy grinned and shook his head. His dark hair was shoulder-length, gleaming. "All gone. Every dime."

"I heard you bought your mother a new double-wide," I said, watching a circle of yellow leaves swirl across the parking lot.

"You'll have more in no time," Perry nodded to him, "won't you?"

"The doctor says for six weeks I'm supposed to use my head strictly for thinking, not for a punching bag."

"And is that what you're going to do?" Perry asked him.

Duncan shrugged. "There's this half-ton pickup over in Newport a guy wants to sell me. It's only two years old. Runs like a dream."

"Trucks!" Perry raised himself higher. "Trucks grow on trees!" He rubbed his thigh, turning his bad leg back and forth, grimacing.

Duncan stood up. Perry's voice was loud. He let go a bit of a song with a sweet Tennessee twang. *Oh, Mr. Half-ton, you come in the mail. They're askin' for full price, but you want it on sale.*

Duncan smiled at me, then stepped back a step toward the door.

Perry went on singing. *High-octane pumpin' all round in your head. Oh, Mr. Half-ton, that's your daily bread.* What was that? Surely not an Elvis song?

After Duncan left, I stood listening to the I.V. leak into Perry with a high-pitched ping, like raindrops—almost ice—smacking the window. It was a tiny fife's accompaniment to Perry's voice, which was no longer Elvis's. Not low or tremulous, but still sure and soft and sweet. It was Perry's voice—the voice I'd hear and those dark eyes I'd see when I shut my own and try to sleep. He should be dead by now, I'd heard a doctor say, but Perry fought. He turned the leg again, going on with the song about the truck. Something in him was standing up. Still singing. It was hard not to love that. But maybe I'd come to my senses if he came to his.

Later, while a nurse swabbed Perry's wound and yet another new doctor scribbled, we'd all rolled our eyes, never sure how much to believe of Perry's stories, his wild Elvis exploits. In this one, he and eleven Navy buddies, all Elvises, had chipped in together for lottery tickets. A hundred tickets. Perry laughed as he talked, his eyes half-closed.

The new doctor bent down and frowned at the leg, then turned to the rest of us. He opened his palms. "I don't know what else."

"I'm going to buy you a Lamborghini," Perry told the doctor, "a red one, if you can save that foot."

The doctor turned and stared at Perry. He nodded. "Good. Red's my color."

Two days later Gladys grabbed my hand in the hallway. "I hear they've got their knives all sharpened up." She reeked of smoke. She'd just come downstairs from having a cigarette on the roof, and now her mouth was chewing loudly, working even more of that fake nicotine from the gum. "Oh Francie," she said.

In his room, Perry told the circle of nurses around him that his job was as demanding as any job. "You put on the uniform and you go to work." He dropped his head back hard on the pillow as the dressing came off his leg. The smell made us all blink. He was describing a candlelight vigil in Graceland. Old ladies whose powdered faces begged a kiss— not from him, no sir, but from the old ghost. The veritable king of kings.

*   *   *

When I saw the line of their five little heads coming up Canyon Road, I knew what they wanted. "Mom," I called across the kitchen, "it's your pals."

She pushed herself forward in the recliner and it snapped closed under her. "I haven't even had my coffee yet."

"Yeah, you have."

She stood up slowly. "Are you sure?"

I nodded and swung open the back door. Ever since Elvis had landed in the hospital six weeks ago, my mother swore she could see his face in a gray rock up the road. On one of our walks she led me to it. She traced her finger around jagged spurs she claimed were the waves of his hair, then over a ridge of silvery mica she couldn't believe I couldn't plainly see was his perfectly curved chin.

"Is it a profile?"

"Hell no, it's the full-on front of his face."

"Is Granny here?" the oldest girl, Marnie, asked me at the door. Then she called into the house, past me, toward my mother. "Gran, it's Saturday."

My mother was still standing by her chair, watching me at the door. She's told me she likes baby-sitting the girls. But if you asked the girls, they'd tell you they're baby-sitting her. No one's wrong, and no one's right.

"You have to put your shoes on, Mom, if you're going out."

"I know, I know." She headed for her bedroom, across the hall from mine.

"Why can't you just trust it, Francie?" she'd asked me last night. "Sometimes love'll happen this way—why not?— right out of the blue."

In the driveway the other four little girls were examining pebbles in the gravel. The smallest one, Erin, was swinging a blue glass telephone insulator on a thick black wire.

"What are you girls up to today?" I asked.

Marnie pointed up Canyon Road to the community lodge. "We're building a yard sculpture. With the Elvis rock. My father's making cement."

"Is it true they cut off Elvis's foot?" another girl, Kiki, asked from her squatting position in the driveway.

I nodded.

"That's a sad story, isn't it?" my mother said, squeezing past me, in an old pair of my rope sandals, out the door. Marnie took her hand.

I was never new to the Farm. Never a stranger dropped in their midst. It seemed I'd simply been away—in another life that was finally over, everything dissolved from the past—and now I was back. Home. They already knew my name. Oh yes, you're Francine. Can you give me a hand cleaning potatoes?

At first I lived for a few months in the lodge, slept in a bunk there. I worked my aide job in town, visited my mother in her trailerhouse in Newport, and during evenings at the Farm, I put on cotton gloves and polished apples. Sometimes I felt I was living in three completely different worlds. One night I was so tired, I lay down in the cool meadow grass. My mother's doctor had been telling me she should go up to Kettle Falls, to the nursing home.

"I've seen those homes," I said to him. "I know what happens there. She's been shuttled to strange places all her life. Enough's enough."

With some help from my neighbors, we towed my mother's trailerhouse up Canyon Road. Then *off* the road. A tan box on a dozen concrete blocks in the cheatgrass.

"I wish they could get rid of the crapola that's eating my brain just like they got rid of what was eating Elvis," my mother said last week. She simulated a shark's jaw with her hand, taking big bites out of the air between us.

"You mean chop out your brain, Mom?"

"No, Francie, like I said, just the icky part."

*   *   *

Perry's leg was a white bundle resting on a pillow, and the doctor-of-the-week lay stretched out on the other bed, his arms crossed behind his head. For the last few days, this was how I'd find them. Watching the science channel. Not much to buy, thank God, on that one. Like Perry, the doctor sipped Coke from a twisty straw in a can. I'd pull up a chair and feed Perry soup, Jell-O, and cheesecake. The doctor liked to watch a program with the latest satellite images of a comet, which resembled a string of raggedy pearls, each with its own grayish halo and tiny tail. The comet was making a beeline for Jupiter.

Perry kept trying to wave my spoon away. "You'll never marry me now, will you, Francie? Not now." He didn't bother whispering anymore.

Sometimes the doctor turned, propped himself on an elbow, and stared at me, then lay back down.

The I.V. pinged into Perry. The comet plummeted into

Jupiter's dark side, impacting like a bomb and sending a mushroom of dust into the Jovian atmosphere.

"Nothing's out of the question," I'd whisper.

Then he'd take another bite of green Jell-O, nibbling at the bright yellow peach that had been sealed inside like a secret.

*   *   *

The geese flew in an enormous jagged V across the canyon, over the frost-nipped yellow scrub brush. The geese honked. Already they seemed tired, but they'd only just started out, and they had a couple thousand miles to go.

My mother and the five little girls waved to the geese. *Honk, honk,* they called upward, their voices and the geese squawks mingling. We were all watching the sky—because it was Sunday, the Farm's final Harvest Potluck, and because I'd promised my neighbors a surprise. Just watch the sky, I'd said.

My mother told everyone she didn't give a hoot whatever the hell her daughter's surprise was, she already had the very most special treat of all: Elvis. Right here among us. She showed Perry the monument, a three-foot high pyramid she and the girls had made out of cement, quartz pebbles, creek rocks, broken glass, a blue telephone insulator, and the whole thing topped off with the Elvis rock.

Perry followed on his crutches, two blond girls right behind him, carrying a folding lawn chair, which they kept opening for him to sit on. But he just smiled and shook his head at the chair. He bent close to the Elvis rock. "Well, would you look at that lopsided sneer," I heard him say to my mother. "That's him, all right, I'd know that nose anywhere."

Both of the long picnic tables were loaded with food. Sonny, Alison, and Roxanne had brought vegetable casseroles. Melody and Leigh had made loaves of bread. Jeannette had brought homemade pickles and beets. Acorn squash, sliced in half, roasted on coals in the fire.

At four o'clock, the appointed hour, Duncan Farrow drove up Canyon Road, honked, and stepped out of his red pickup. Ann Marie got out the other door. They both stood for a moment, smiling at the barefoot softball players in the field. "I've got it, Francine," Duncan called. "Fresh. Ain't even been froze." His long hair blew behind him in the breeze.

I helped him unload the foil-wrapped packages. Where a few had leaked into the middle of the truck bed, a dark pool of blood glistened. This was, as I'd promised my mother, the meat. Let the others turn up their noses. Blast the unwritten rules meant to keep us on the vegetarian track. This was a big black moose, by god.

Duncan had been happy to sell it to Perry and me. "We've got to have us some steaks," Perry had said, "the real thing, to feed the gathering crowds." Besides, the deal he'd made with Duncan was, as he said, a win-win. The price of Duncan's moose was the exact down payment for the snazzy red pickup.

Now the moose sizzled on the fire. "God love it," my mother said, sniffing the air. The moose was a sumptuous dream of sweet dark flesh proffered by the Hoodoo Mountains and brought down by a young man with a bow and arrow in the old way. "Sit down," she said to Perry. "Sit yourself down now."

"They got pretty girls up here. You bet," I'd heard him tell his friends on the phone. "Fly on up. They'll love you to pieces." He had laughed into the receiver. "Don't forget, my right leg's a foot short."

"Sometimes I *do* forget," was what he said to me when we were alone. "I take a step and think my other foot's going to set itself down like always. But then no. No siree."

In the lawn chair Perry rolled up his silky white shirt sleeves. The I.V.'s purple bruise on the inside of his arm had dimmed to yellow. Everyone wanted to touch the soft, delicate fringe around his shirt pockets.

Geneva arrived and passed out cold bottles of imported beer. Everyone smiled and admired the pretty blue embossed labels. Sonny and Roxanne were going around reminding people that the "special" brownies, contributed by Scooter and Don, were not for consumption by the small fry.

I'd told Perry we could announce *not* our impending marriage but only an engagement. "There's a big difference," I said. "We can stay *engaged* forever. Why not?"

"Till the cows come home."

"Then, when you clear all the drugs out of your body, you can change your mind if you want. You might. When you get your life back."

"When I get back on my foot."

I handed a plate of moose and squash to my mother,

and she squinted down at it. She touched the meat with one finger. "What is that?"

"A steak. Moose."

Two little girls on either side of her strained their heads up to see the top of the plate. "I'm getting some of that," Jess, the smaller, freckled-face one, said and took off on a run. The other girl watched my mother.

"No, I don't think so." My mother smiled politely at me and handed the plate back. "My daughter doesn't like me to eat meat."

"It's okay," I told her. "Really. She said it was fine."

Just then the plane appeared. Everyone looked up. It roared through the canyon, between the two ridgetops.

I knelt down and kissed Perry's ear. He had on his Elvis wig, which smelled smoky from a thousand saloons and nightclubs.

"I've got a million bucks in the bank, baby," he whispered and tipped his head back in the chair. "But the beauty of you is, see, the beauty is, you aren't ever in a buying mood. Am I right?" He watched the plane.

When it reached one end of the canyon, it banked and circled back. The two girls who'd been taking turns trying to walk with Perry's crutches let them fall. They stared up. Everyone did. Rollie took off his straw hat and waved it to the sky.

"Hey! Listen up now," Marnie shouted into the crowd as she and I helped Perry stand. His hand trembled slightly against my shoulder.

"Darlin' girls, could you pass me my helpers?" Perry called to the little blonds, and they carefully put the crutches under his arms.

"What I lost," he began, "is more than made up for by what I found. This good woman, Francine, she's agreed to get herself engaged to me."

"Oh golly," my mother said. Her eyes welled up.

We were besieged with hugs and applause. The plane had climbed; its engine noise was a soft drone.

"Okay." Perry nodded to me. "Hit it."

I leaned down and punched "play" on Perry's boombox. *Well, bless-a my soul, what's wrong with me? I'm itchin' like a man on a fuzzy tree.*

Suddenly, above the canyon walls, several white ovals began falling from the plane's belly.

"Turn up the music." Perry took a few zigzag strides on his crutches.

Marnie bent and turned up the volume. *Friends say I'm actin' wild as a bug.* Down below everyone was bopping. Kicking up their legs. *I'm proud to say she's my buttercup.*

As the plane passed out of sight, the white shapes in the sky stretched from ovals into lines, into bodies. Into men. Eleven men. Dropping down.

The men fell toward us, and as they did, they drifted— as if blown by the winds—into a circle, joining hands. Then pop, pop, pop, and swoosh!—their chutes opened.

And *Whoa, I'm in love. I'm all shook up.*

All at once, we could hear them, the Flying Elvi,

singing. Their song rained down as the kings descended. The white chutes swirled above us, above the wonderful odors of orange squash and seared meat.

On his crutches Perry propelled himself out past the fire pit toward the newly hoed potato field where the men were touching down. He sang too—softly, one voice among the dozen.

Each of the Elvises—wearing white suits like his, even the same white shoes—hit the earth running, dragging the cords and the silk through the fresh dirt. Then they stepped out of their chutes, left them, and came toward us, toward the tables of food. The eleven men hurried, waving and brushing out the fringe on their shirts. The bass guitar on the boombox deepened our heartbeats.

Two little girls were leading my mother out into the field. She looked around, dazed. She seemed to have lost herself in the excitement. She hung on to the girls' hands and let them take her. They were her daughters, I saw then, as much as I was. They were the first to greet the Flying Elvi.

Each Elvis kissed each cheek he was offered—kissing and trying to continue forward at the same time, to get to what sizzled on the fire. My mother straightened one of the Elvis's wigs and smiled her approval. The men's white shoes traipsed through the black soil. These were the hungry Elvises. They licked their lips.